Targeted-
An Isaac Jones Thriller ©

By Ryan Pacheco and Dennis Mansfield

Library of Congress Cataloging-in-Publication Data
Pacheco, Ryan/ Mansfield, Dennis -
Targeted-An Isaac Jones Thriller

ISBN-10: 0-692-70099-4
ISBN-13: 978-0-692-70099-0 – Electronic book format

Cover Art Work by Lindy Bronson

Cover Design by 10-41
Cover Art used by permission

Printed in the United States of America
First Edition

Ryan Pacheco
Acknowledgments

For my mother, Susie, with love

In 2012 I began writing my first novel and in 2013 my friend Dennis Mansfield came on board. In 2014, that project became, Benghazi and Beyond- An Isaac Jones Thriller and was published. The reception was warm and sales continue to do well. I refer to it as the little book that could. Like the little train that could, Benghazi continues to chug along. How cool is that? In 2015 I released my first solo effort, The Heist- An Alexander Stone Thriller and later the first two parts of my Young Adult series, Earth's Dimensions. I also began work on Targeted, the second book in the Isaac Jones series, which you are now holding. I love writing the characters in this series. You could say they have become almost like extended family and I love where they take me as I write their stories. I look forward to exploring the possibilities of where they can take us next. I know this book has been a long time coming and I hope you enjoy it as much as we enjoyed writing it. Strap in, here we go.

Thank you to my friends at the ACSO, The Idaho ICAC-TF, Galen Fields, Jay Gustavsen my one man legal team, Jeff Anderson, David Day, Gary Raney, Clay Buie, what an inspiration you are, my friends at the Idaho DHW,10-41 publishing, Sofa Press, Dennis and Susan Mansfield, Hannah and Colin Mansfield, Lindy Bronson for another great cover, Mark Halley my editor and to all who continue to read my stories and encourage me through kind words.

To my family in Idaho, California, and Texas whose love and support never fails me. To Tauna for continued support and love. Zachary, Chaz, Rylan, Rachel, Terry Lynn, Gene and Vikki, Laz, Jenny & Dirk, Regina & Jeff, Justin & Jeannie, Patty Kubitschek, Dan, Rich, Rod, Robert, Vanessa, Kristi, Rick & Cindi, Ray & Rose, Susan Habeler, Isaac, Olive, and Lillianna.

Dennis Mansfield
Acknowledgments

To my bride Susan, who long ago encouraged me to write with authority.
To Caleb and Colin for serving in the United States Military; and to Meg and Hannah for supporting their men as they protect and serve.
To Cole and Amelia for giving all of us hope for the future.

Chapter 1

The less-than-subtle pulsing ringtone of Led Zeppelin's "Immigrant Song" eventually awakens Isaac Jones from a deep sleep.

At first, the ringtone seems part of a strange dream that has some type of running, leaping, and then, flying...the type of dream that seems impossible, unless you're the one flying. The third ring grounds him, and his eyes slowly open.

Jones, a West Point Graduate, Army Ranger, and CIA black asset, officially doesn't exist. The only people who know he traffics in covert missions on behalf of the United States Government is Deputy Director of Clandestine Operations, Steven Waxman, Waxman's assistant, Stella, Congressman Raul Lopez, and Senator James Thurston. Not even Waxman's boss, Assistant Director of the CIA, Trent McBride, knows of Jones' real work for the CIA. Lately, McBride has become less of a fan of Jones' off-the-radar movements.

Jones rolls over slightly in bed and painfully squints at the clock on the nightstand. He rubs the sleep from his eyes...3:23a.m. Recognizing the number calling him, he reaches for the phone. "This better be important, she knows it's the middle of the night here," he mumbles to no one. Using his finger, he slides the lock across the iPhone's screen and holds it to his ear.

"Yon, everything ok?" he asks with a sleepy but concerned voice.

"Isaac, you've got to get out of there!" he barely hears the whispered words from her winded voice. It sounds like she's running.

"Wha... What's wrong?" he shakes the sleep from his head.

"They're after me and I think they are coming for you. Get out of there! Go dark–" She's interrupted by the sounds of gunfire so loud Jones pulls the phone away from his ear. The line goes dead.

"Yon? Yon!" No answer.

Jones bolts up, swinging his legs off the edge of the bed, with adrenalin from the strange call starting to pump through his body. Jones is a strong man, both in stature *and* personality. At 6'0" tall and 180 pounds, he's in the best shape of his life. He's pensive and quietly handsome. He doesn't stand out in a crowd, and he doesn't want to – unless conditions demand he do so.

He wears a St. Michael pendant around his neck, attached to a gold chain, a gift from his godfather, former CIA Director Ethan Christensen. More an "uncle" than a former employer, Christensen personally invested himself in Isaac Jones – and the younger man's career didn't suffer because of it, either.

Jones is a man of faith, though he doesn't regularly attend church services. If asked, he would say he's a Christian and leave it at that. To him, discussing religion, like politics, is the worst possible conversation killer, so he keeps out of the debates.

He has thick dark hair combed back, slightly off his forehead. He used to wear it military-short, but now, since being assigned to the CIA, he lets it grow out longer and keeps it well-managed. He tans easily in the summer, and his skin lightens-up considerably in the winter. His unique gait is somewhat striking, something between John Wayne and Clint Eastwood. When in the thick of action, his intimidating stride intensifies.

He stares at the dead phone and redials Yon's number. It goes directly to voicemail. He grabs the t-shirt he left on the end of the bed the previous night, slips it on and climbs into the pair of jeans he left lying on the floor. Reaching over to the small nightstand, he opens a small drawer, grabbing his 9-mm Glock handgun. He pulls back the slide, confirming that a round is chambered. His training kicks-in: check your equipment before you go to work.

Barefooted, he holds the gun up in front of him, scanning from the bedroom window, then down the hallway. Like a cat on the prowl, he bends slightly, moving quickly into the hallway checking first to the left, then to the right, with his handgun leading the way. It's clear…no trace of anyone. He slowly and silently traverses to the end of the hallway, then into the living room. It's dark, but he knows the layout. He looks to the windows for signs of shadows or movement. Nothing.

Confused, he tries to gather his thoughts. Should he report this to his boss, CIA Deputy Director Waxman, or figure this out himself? What would he tell Waxman? All he knows is Yon had said someone was after her and thought they might come for him next. Yon's work on behalf of South Korea's National Intelligence Service supports his trust in her. Not long ago, she and Jones teamed up on a covert mission in North Korea. When she speaks, he listens.

Jones thinks to himself, *What do we really know? Nothing.*

Out of the silence, the sound of shattering glass shakes him from his thoughts. He instantly spins around and faces the living room windows. Then he feels a crushing sensation, as if his chest is caving-in. He loses balance and falls backward to the ground, landing on his back. The back of his head strikes the hardwood floor forcefully, causing disorientation, and making him lose his grip on the Glock. He turns his head, looking for his pistol...it's on the ground but out of reach. His hands instinctively go to his chest, scanning for signs of entry wounds or blood. Finding neither, he withdraws his hands and tries to catch his breath. One hand falls to the floor on something small and round, but hard. He picks it up, holding it close to his eyes, trying to focus. A rubber bullet round? Confusion sets in. He hears the house phone ring.

Jones is unsettled. Normally, he's almost always on the alert, but being attacked, and at home, leaves him at a loss. He silently curses himself for allowing himself to be in this situation. He let down his guard. "What a fool! Big mistake!" he mumbles to himself. He had allowed himself to be compromised by not following his own set of rules: *Always be aware of possible threats, and always be prepared to fight. Above all, stay alive!* Now, he wonders if this lapse of judgment will be his last. *Not if I can help it! Get to work, get off your ass and fight!* he tells himself.

As he sits up, chest still aching, a half-dozen men breach the front door holding automatic rifles with red laser targeting, all sighted on Jones; he's lit up with red dots and the corresponding laser lines, highlighting the dust lingering in the air. The men grab Jones, pushing him over onto his stomach. He's still too disoriented to give much of a fight. They bind his wrists and feet with plastic zip-tie cuffs, gag his mouth, and cover his face with a cloth hood. Jones struggles to break free, but he's hopelessly outnumbered. He receives a paralyzing blow to the head, a signal to stop the struggle. The men pull him to his feet. Jones feels someone pull up the sleeve of his t-shirt then a sharp sting in his arm. *They're drugging me, not good,* he thinks, as his shoulder starts to burn. The burning sensation moves up his neck and his cheeks become warm and his mouth goes dry. His last thoughts before passing-out from the injection is, *these are pros, but...who?*

The men pull Jones out of the house by his armpits, letting his feet slide on the ground behind him. They make their way across the lawn and sidewalk to a non-descript industrial van parked on the side of the house, near the street. The van's sliding side door opens, and Jones gets tossed inside like a bag of potatoes, then the door slams closed.

From the street, a shot fires in the direction of the van, spraying a circle of small holes into the back of the doors, leaving the pattern of a 16-gauge shotgun load with a fairly tight choke. The men drop to their knees, facing the threat and respond with a volley of automatic shots. They see the shadow of a figure duck behind a tree. They jump into the van and speed-off with a squeal of tires into the black night, leaving behind the smell of burnt rubber in a cloud of smoke. The figure peers out from around the tree, holding the shotgun close to his chest, with anger in his eyes. This man is Jones' elderly neighbor, Eldon Chase.

Eldon is a neighborly guy, and yet, not really a friend to Jones, more like an acquaintance. He's a pastor at a small church in town. Having lost his wife just a few years before

to cancer, the widower always seems lonely. Most of the conversations he's had with Jones happen through a fence, usually with Chase ending the conversation with a small sermon of biblical advice, which Jones has grown to value. Though ageing,
Chase is still a strong man with a strong will. But tonight, as the remaining smoke vanishes into thin air, Chase looks down the street, now quiet and dark, with defeat on his face.

WASHINGTON, D.C.

CIA Deputy Director Waxman awakens from a deep, restful sleep to the sound of his phone ringing. He looks at the clock on the nightstand, 3:25a.m.

"This better be good," he answers with irritation.

"Sir, this is Bartlett with Asset Security. We've received a breach alarm at one of the asset safe houses. We called the location, got

no answer. Sorry to bother you, but the instructions say you are to be notified immediately."

"What? Which house?" he yawns, trying to wake-up.

"Boise, Idaho."

"Jones? Are you sure?"

"Sir, as protocol, we checked for a malfunction and found none. It's still sending the breach alarm, and like I said, there's no answer when we call."

"Get someone over there immediately!" Waxman is now fully awake. His concern is that only a handful of people even know about Jones and the safe house in Boise.

"Sir, the instructions say 'no local law enforcement involvement.'"

"Who do we have in the area?"

"The closest team is at Mountain Home AFB. It's about ten minutes by chopper. I need your authorization to activate them."

"Do it! Do it now! I'm on my way in."

Chapter 2

Nathan Mitchell loves being called "Mr. President." After taking the oath of office six months ago, the first one to call him by the most famous title in the world was his wife and the love of his life, Tabitha, right on the steps of the National Mall in front of the world. No sooner had he put his right hand down after swearing his oath, she walked over and embraced him, whispering in his ear, "Congratulations, Mr. President!" It sent chills down his spine. Over the past six months he's heard the title thousands of times, and he still gets pumped. He worked hard to gain the position as the nation's chief executive. Even more, he believes he's still the best man for the job.

He's known his wife since junior high. They dated all through high school, and they married in their first year of college, without hesitation on their part, however, both of their parents were uncertain, and though they should each finish college first. Ahh, but they were in love, and still are today, thirty years later.

Mitchell just celebrated his fiftieth birthday and his wife will celebrate hers next year. He is a towering figure, standing 6'2" tall, and 175 pounds. He's in good shape, and works-out on a regular basis, mostly swimming and riding his mountain bike. Thought his dark hair has started to lightly sprinkle with grey specks around his temples, he looks ten years younger than he actually is. 'Old school handsome' is the description many give him, which didn't hurt him at all during the elections. He won the female vote by almost 65%, with support from both sides of the political spectrum. He's very comfortable in his own skin, and confident of his politics. He kisses babies, but refrains from kissing butts - often to the annoyance of his staff, saying, "If they don't like my position, they can vote for the other guy."

After college, he and his wife opened a shipping business in the southwest, much like Federal Express or UPS, but on a smaller scale. Over the years, they franchised Mitchell Shipping, adding over 500 stores throughout the United States, becoming a powerhouse, and eventually even rivaling the big dogs, branding the company with the simple phrase, "Mitchell Can." In his run for President, they used the same mantra and the American people believed it. Some have estimated his wealth to be over $400 million. If asked, he would simply say, "We do pretty well." One thing he learned from Mitt Romney's failed presidential bid was to not act embarrassed by his success and to NEVER apologize for it. Rather, "Embracing hard work is living the American dream, a dream anyone can obtain. Success follows." The saying emanates from him, almost like breathing.

After years of stagnant wages, high unemployment, economic uncertainty, and dwindling foreign policy strength, Americans were hungry for leadership. They wanted a beacon of hope and strength. They found it in Nathan Mitchell.

And don't underestimate Tabitha Mitchell. She is just as sharp as her husband. Much shorter than her husband, standing only 5'6" tall, she has an alluring elegance with long, light brown hair, worn in loose curls, which complement her caramel-colored eyes. She wears red lipstick that accentuates her almost pouty, but sensual, lips. She's a smart dresser, mostly pant suits, but can dress-up a gown when the occasion calls for it. Hollywood loves her classy demeanor, yet she remains approachable. She is her husband's first advisor, but chooses to not be overly engaged in policy like Hillary Clinton was as First Lady.

Earlier in the day, President Mitchell sat in the Oval Office with his Chief of Staff, Giovanni Harrison, referred to by the President as "Gio." Harrison has been with Mitchell since his first run for the Senate in the State of California a dozen years ago. After two terms in the Senate, and now in the Oval Office, the two men are more than trusted friends, they consider themselves family. Harrison has none of the outward charisma his boss has. He's not considered good looking, being rather scrawny and rumpled. He has thinning brown hair pulled over his round head, not quite bald, but his scalp is visible, and it never seems neatly combed. Some have the opinion that he looks out of place in the White House. He doesn't care. He *is* the Chief of Staff to the President of the United States. Although his appearance is non-descript, everyone knows this man has the President's ear, and that he is a formidable strategist. No one wants to be on his bad side. Gio does the President's difficult duties, and more times than not, he gets the President what he wants.

The two men had scheduled this hour for a discussion they've been putting-off since the swearing-in: what to do with the CIA? The most recent Director resigned months ago, correctly anticipating that the new administration would replace him. That seat has been sitting unoccupied far too long. It is time to nominate a new head spy for the United States.

18

The President is looking at a list of names provided to him as possible candidates. He put his hand to his forehead in thought, "What do you say we pick this up tomorrow?"

"Yes, Mr. President," his Chief of Staff answered, thinking, this is the third time they have put the decision off. It needs to be addressed; however, Gio respects his boss's wish.

LANGLEY, VIRGINIA

Deputy Director Steven Waxman oversees the CIA's national clandestine operations with responsibilities ranging from all covert operations to collecting foreign intelligence. He's a former Army Ranger who joined the CIA in the 90's. He's above-average in height, with salt-&-pepper hair. He has a tough look that's offset by his soft, brown eyes.

His driver picks him up in a blacked-out Suburban within minutes of requesting a transport to the CIA airport hangar. He jumps in the back seat quickly before the driver even had a chance to get out and open the door for him. "Let's go!"

Ten minutes later the Suburban, with its blue emergency lights flashing, pulls up on the tarmac next to a CIA Executive Jet Gulfstream IV, already fueled and ready to go. The door is open, and the stairs are in position. Waxman lets himself out and rushes up the stairs, Henry, the one-man flight crew, appears atop the stairs, welcoming his VIP. Henry is assigned to this specific jet and travels with it…everywhere. He's an interesting looking young man in his late 20's, with short, spiky, black hair, reminiscent of a 90's garage band singer. In the past, he accompanied Isaac

Jones on assignments in this very jet, and they become valued friends. Today, dressed in his black pants and white, heavily-starched shirt, the worried look on his face reveals the same emotion Waxman has been trying to hide.

Henry has flown all over the world, shuttling CIA assets in and out of danger spots over his five years with the Agency. But Jones was the first asset he became friends with. For some reason, they "clicked," and to this day, they have a solid bond of friendship.

"Sir," Henry addresses Waxman as he reaches the top of the stairs.

"Let's get moving, Henry. I want to be in the air five minutes ago," Waxman says as he steps inside and grabs the first seat he comes to, setting his laptop bag in the seat next to him.

"Yes, sir!" The stairs are pulled away, the door shuts, and the cabin secured for takeoff. They are, in fact, in the air in less than five minutes.

Henry pours Waxman a cup of coffee and delivers it saying, "Sir, Ms. Stella asked that you call her on a secure video conference when you can."

"Thank you, Henry," he states simply, taking the coffee cup, lifting it to his mouth. Waxman sits back, setting the cup in its carriage, and squeezes his eyes shut tightly, attempting to deny the onset of a migraine. *What in the heck is going on?* he wonders to himself.

After the North Korean mission, where Jones and Yon destroyed North Korea's Missile and Drone Command Center, Waxman's boss, Assistant CIA Director, Trent

McBride, started asking questions about the incidents, and had particular interest in Jones. Longing to be "in the know". McBride asked questions long before then, but it was the North Korean mission that raised scrutiny. Senator Thurston, Congressman Lopez, and Waxman had collectively decided to keep McBride out of the loop on Jones' missions because they didn't know if he could be trusted. McBride was an outsider, appointed to his post, rather than working his way up in the Agency. Waxman has provided only cursory information, but McBride continues to dig.

Waxman, his executive assistant, Ms. Stella, Sen. Thurston, Rep. Lopez, Henry, and Jones' outsourced team are the only ones that know about these black missions. However, former CIA Director Christensen, who still knows everything going on in D.C., seems to have figured it out. This creates mild irritation for Waxman, Thurston and Lopez, not because Christensen can't keep his mouth shut, but because he's Jones' Godfather, and that gives him skin in the game.

Waxman's thoughts suddenly snap back to wondering what happened at Jones' safe house. He's anxious to land and talk with Jones' neighbor. Unbeknownst to Jones, Eldon Chase is a retired CIA asset, and now a black location guardian. Chase's job is to keep an eye on the safe house while the asset is traveling, and more importantly, to keep an eye on the mental health of the asset when at home.

Chapter 3

Isaac Jones forces his eyes shut, out of utter irritation. *How stupid could I be? I should never have let my guard down!* he swears at himself. Although he is slowly coming around, the drugs injected into him are still causing him to feel disoriented. He wonders how long he's been out, and how long they've been traveling with him bound in the back of the van. Even though the hood has been yanked off his head, he purposely lays completely still, hoping to catch the men in conversation. Perhaps he'll hear them talking about why they grabbed him or where they are going. Maybe, if they have an accent, he'll be able to figure-out even more. Being a man who thrives on being in charge, he detests the position he's now in. The tables have indeed turned on him –now that he is the one taken down… and it's his own fault. He knows it, and doesn't like that he knows it.

Time passes, and Jones is frustrated that the men haven't said a word. As his head clears-up, he thinks of Yon, who tried to alert him to all this, and hopes she is alright. His mind is whirling, his thoughts turning… *Is this the same group that was after Yon? This can't be a coincidence. Did they get her, or is she still on the run? If they nabbed her, are they taking me to wherever they have her? Damn, this sucks! Clear your head and think!*

The rushing thoughts are pummeling him. He checks his wrists for any give, but the bindings are tight and unyielding.

Jones feels the van pull off the pavement, onto some type of dirt area, then back onto pavement, finally coming to a stop. Silently, the men get out. Three sets of arms carry Jones out of the van. He keeps his eyes closed pretending to still be drugged. The cool air on his face is refreshing. He smells the sweet scent of rain before being overwhelmed by the pungent odor of jet fuel. *Airport*, Jones concludes. He slightly opens one eye and catches a glimpse of what seems to be a small industrial airport, but he doesn't recognize it. Aside from his captors, it appears deserted. *Nighttime at an airport is always lonely*, he thinks.

The men carry him up some stairs into a small plane, and place him on the floor between the seats. Jones hears someone kneel down next to him, and feels a sting on his neck, then warmth fills his face. *Here we go again*, he thinks just as the world goes dark.

What Jones doesn't know is that this flight is bound for Seattle, and then from Seattle to Valdez, Alaska, where a cargo ship is waiting for him. It's now after 4:00a.m.

****

Deputy Director Waxman taps his finger nervously on the armrest of his seat. Henry refreshes his coffee. As he pours, Henry says, "Sir, Ms. Stella is still trying to reach you on the secure video conference."

"Thanks, Henry." Waxman grabs his laptop from the next seat, placing it on his bent knees. He knew Stella would take

24

the capture of Jones difficult. Over time, Jones and she have become close. *It's difficult not to,* he thinks to himself. As he lifts the lid and the screen powers up, he sees the alert in the top corner that a conference is waiting for him to join. He clicks the tab and sees his assistant's empty desk, and then she walks into view, taking a seat in front of her computer.

Strikingly beautiful, with soft, blond hair that falls just past her shoulders, Ms. Stella moved from London to Washington, D.C. nearly ten years ago to attend a local university. As a struggling college student, she applied for a paid internship at the CIA as a part of her political science degree. After passing a lengthy, and obviously intrusive, background check, she was granted low-level access employment. Before long, she found working for America's premier spy agency to be, as she would say, "lovely." After completing her Bachelors degree, she was urged by her superiors to come to work for the Agency full-time. She applied to be the executive assistant for then-Director of CIA, Ethan Christensen. The competition was fierce. So, she was surprised when she got the nod for the job, and loved every minute of working for the man she playfully called "The Old Dog." After Christensen retired, she went to work for her current boss, Steven Waxman. It's not as glamorous a position as being the executive assistant to the Director, but she has grown to respect and appreciate working for Waxman.

Not quite 30, she has wisdom far beyond her years. She's seen enough in her time at the Agency to separate political truth from reality. She knows all too well that in Washington, D.C., the politically correct "truth" often overrules actual reality. There are plenty of grey areas presented to an American public that wants "black-and-white".

Her no-nonsense British nationality and personality also makes her perfect for her job, and Waxman likes to say she balances his over-serious American nature.

She and Isaac Jones work closely together since most of the time she gives him his operational instructions and support. Often, the two playfully tease each other and care about each other, but it's purely professional. She knows Jones and Yon developed a romantic relationship during the North Korean mission, though she doesn't know if that relationship has developed into something serious. And although she finds Jones engaging and handsome, she's fine with her own current friendship with him...and his with her.

Waxman thinks Stella looks tired as she takes a seat in front of her monitor. Her eyes are bloodshot, as if she's been crying, and she isn't dressed in her normal business suit, but rather in jeans and a grey sweatshirt, with her hair pulled back in a ponytail.

"Sir."

"Good morning, Stella."

"Is he alright?"

"We don't know yet. He's still missing."

"Bugger!" She takes a deep breath. "I came in as soon as I heard. Your phone has been ringing. Senator Thurston and Congressman Lopez have asked that you make contact A.S.A.P and..." she pauses.

"What, Stella?"

"Ethan Christensen has called twice. I didn't tell him anything but he already seems to know something has happened to Isaac."

"I'm not surprised. He still seems to know most everything that goes on in this town."

"Yes, sir, I know. And what about Jones' son, Michael? He's at the boarding school, but what will we do if something has happened to his father?"

In Germany, during the Reagan mission, Jones saved a young boy from martyring himself with a suicide vest. Jones brought the boy back to America, adopted him, and placed him in the same school that his godfather, Ethan Christensen, had placed him in as a boy after his mother died, West Nottingham Academy, the oldest and one of the most prestigious boarding schools in America.

"Michael doesn't need to know anything right now, Stella. Set up a conference with Thurston and Lopez, and I'll call Ethan after."

"Alright."

"Have you been watching to see if he activated his tracker…the one we put in after he returned from the Reagan mission?" Waxman asks.

"Of course I've been watching. Nothing is transmitting."

"Okay, and Stella…"

"Yes?"

27

"Call General Mooney. See if he happened to have a bird covering that area. Maybe we'll get lucky."

"I'll do that straight away."

Chapter 4

"How could this happen, Steven?" Senator Thurston demands. Thurston's burrowing eyes, sheltered by his boxy forehead, are intently staring at Deputy Director Waxman via the encrypted videoconference. Thurston is an old-guard, establishment, career politician who's been in the Senate longer than most. He's 5'8", with a 42-inch waist that he's been unsuccessfully attempting to reduce. He has puffy lips like Mick Jagger and he's a member of the Democratic Party, elected from the State of Vermont, and sits on the Senate Committee on Foreign Relations and the Senate Homeland Security and Governmental Affairs Committee.

"Senator, we don't have all the information yet. I should land at Mountain Home shortly," Waxman replies.

"I thought we had a man keeping an eye on the house, Steven." Congressman Lopez states, his face filling-up the other side of Waxman's monitor. Lopez is the opposite of Thurston in demeanor and temperament. He's a ten-term congressman who Thurston still refers to as a "rookie" - compared to his decades inside the Beltway. Over 20 years ago, Lopez was an Army Sergeant and this has made him well-respected by his peers. He has dark hair and darker eyes, and is clean-cut with a handsome, cowboy look. His constituents accepted his Army resume, and continue accepting it, election after election.

"We have a black location guardian living next door to the house, but he's not there for security. He's a retired wet asset. His job is to watch the location when the asset is deployed, and gauge the asset's mental health when he's home, that's it. I mean the man has to be pushing 70 now. I'm surprised he was able to do as much as he did."

"Don't underestimate Chase. He has a history that books are written about. We have to contain this, Steven. Get in, clean it up, and get out. I don't want anyone asking questions. We don't need Jones compromised," directs the Senator.

"I realize that, Senator," Waxman replies, clearly irritated with the Senator stating the obvious. "You can bet McBride is going to be all over me when I return. He's been suspicious of what we've had Jones doing from the start."

"Keep him out of it as best you can, and find Jones. I want every one of those son-of-a-guns eliminated" Thurston growls.

"Now, hold on," Congressman Lopez pipes-up. "We don't even know what happened, or who has him. Let's not talk about killing people we haven't even identified yet."

"Raul, I don't give a rat's ass who it is. They can't covertly grab one of our assets from one of our black sites and expect to get away with it, foreign or domestic!" Thurston yells, his face turning red.

"Calm down, Senator, you're going to pop a vein. All I'm saying is let's slow down and figure-out what happened before we launch a response," Lopez calmly inserts.

"Steven, what are your initial thoughts?"

"Well, it could be someone from his Army Ranger days. Someone who sold him out – and knew how to get to him. It could be Russian's attached to Nicolay Poloski and the Reagan Connection mission; they have always suspected we played a part in the death of their black operative, even if he was working with terrorists. Heck, it could be Iran responding to the Benghazi mission. They have no doubt we hit that safe house hiding the Benghazi terrorists. It could even be North Korea responding to Jones being there. I mean, we blew up their missile and drone control center, and Jones killing that one-eyed solider, Soju, left a serious ripple inside the North Korean government. If you think about it, we've pissed-off a lot of people in a short period of time. We just simply don't know yet. And, how they found Jones' location at the black site is simply beyond me."

"Well, find out!" demands Thurston and his side of the screen goes black.

"Steven, I know you're under a lot of pressure and you're doing your best. Just remember, Jones has a lot of information that, if made public, would cause a firestorm around all of our heads," Lopez cautions.

"I understand. I'll keep you in the loop," replies Waxman. He logs-off, and falls back into his seat with a large sigh.

Henry, noticing Waxman is off the videoconference, approaches with a satellite phone in his hand. "Sir, Ethan Christensen is holding for you."

"And the hits just keep on coming. Thanks, Henry." Taking the phone, he says "Hi, Ethan. Sorry to keep you waiting, it's been a busy morning."

"Steven, I don't have to tell you how concerned I am."

"No, you don't."

"I know you're busy, but I want to know what you know."

Normally Waxman wouldn't give out sensitive information, but Ethan Christensen is the former Director of the CIA, his old boss, and he's a friend. Waxman doesn't even bother to ask how the former Director had found out something happened to his godson; though he's not the Director of the CIA anymore, he's still tapped into what's going on in Washington, D.C. Even now, he's still feared by many. Like his predecessors, there are rumors of secret files in his possession. Those secret files encompass vast high profile people, including celebrities, politicians, businessmen, and judges. People who have skeletons in their closets fear him, particularly the many closets in the nation's capital. He's still a man with a considerable amount of information. And in this town, information is power.

Waxman tells Christensen everything discussed in the videoconference he just had with the Senator and Congressman. Christensen doesn't interrupt.

When Waxman is done, Christensen asks a simple question, "Could it be someone from the inside?"

The question hung in the air.

"From the inside? A double agent?"

"Perhaps."

"You're thinking something else?" Waxman presses.

"Just considering all the possibilities."

"McBride?" Waxman asks, stunned.

"Perhaps."

"I can't believe even McBride would stoop that low. Even if he would, how could he? He doesn't have the assets for a domestic operation like that without someone leaking the information. No one at the Agency likes him. Word would have gotten out."

"Perhaps."

"It would ruin his chances of becoming Director. The President's about to make an announcement on the new head soon, and no matter how bad he wants to get to Jones, there's no way he'd take the risk. I just don't see it."

"You would be surprised what a man's ego would have him do, Steven. Just keep it in the back of your mind. Something stinks here, and Jones is being targeted."

"But, why?"

"That's the million dollar question. Figure that out and you'll find Isaac, hopefully alive. You guys started down a dangerous path when you started the Animus Project. As you said, you've pissed-off a lot of foreign governments and raised suspicion from a lot of powerful people in Washington. You've threatened their sense of importance. Politicians are naturally insecure. Mess around in their backyard, and they take it personally, even if what you're doing is in the best interest of the country. Watch your back, Steven. Grabbing Jones could either be just the beginning, or it could be the means to an end. I'm not sure which, but neither is desirable."

"Understood."

"Steven, I want my godson home. Alive."

"So do I," Waxman replies, as he ends the call. *So do I.*"

THE WHITE HOUSE

President Mitchell and Chief of Staff Harrison are back where they left off the day before. The President is sitting at his desk looking at the names of people for consideration as the new head of the CIA. Harrison is seated in front of him patiently waiting, silently twirling his thumbs around each other.

Mitchell tosses the paper on his desk, "You know, I don't know half these names, Gio."

"Yes, Sir, I'm aware of that, but you asked me to reach out to Congress for suggestions. Those are the suggestions."

"I see Senator Heart likes Trent McBride," the President says with a raised eyebrow.

"I figured you'd notice that one."

The President shakes his head, "She's a piece of work isn't she? And McBride? What a load of crap he is! How in the world he became Assistant Director of the CIA is beyond me.

Everyone knows he's a political hack, and his butt-kissing is an embarrassment."

"He's been approaching members of Congress non-stop since the former Director stepped-down. He's made it clear, he wants the job."

"I'll tell you this," the President sits up, pointing at the paper, "McBride will NEVER be the Director of the CIA. Not on my watch."

"Yes, Sir." Harrison replies, nodding in agreement. "So, scratch one off the list. Only 24 to go."

The President picks up the page, draws a line through Trent McBride's name, and looks up at his Chief of Staff. "Congressman Lopez thinks Steven Waxman would be good. I know Steven. He's testified on the Hill a few times, and we've had lunch together."

"Yes, I know."

"Is he still overseeing our clandestine services?"

"Yes."

"Well, it would be nice to have a spy overseeing our spying," the President smiles, looking over his glasses at Gio.

"Now, there's a novel idea."

"Set up a meeting."

"Yes, Sir."

Chapter 5

There is a small, obscure mountain in the center of the French Alps. Its unassuming peak is not as it appears, having been hollowed-out and reinforced with concrete. The high-tech security is state of the art at keeping out unwanted guests, and because of that, it helps conceal the secret presence. It's simply invisible to the world. This is the headquarters of "COMMON," a secret society in existence for 100 years. "COMMON: *Covert Operations, Missions, & Manipulation Of Nations.*" Each generation of members has believed that the group operates for the *common* good of the world; however, newer members have begun wondering if it's simply about personal wealth and world power. The division among the group is small, yet growing. Many old-guard leaders within COMMON think of the world as a chess game, and *they* decide what pieces to move, which pawns to sacrifice, and which kings and queens get to survive.

As in the cases of the Illuminati and Freemasonry, COMMON has become much more malevolent over time. It has always been comprised of twelve members. Each member, in turn, has a protégé, a member in the making, who assumes his master's seat when the master retires or dies. Protégés are not allowed to attend formal meetings, but are informed of goings-on as their masters see fit.

This group, currently comprised of eight men and four women, has been puppeteering western nations since its onset. Long ago, the group was initially involved in global peace and prosperity. As the world prospers, so would the members of the group. But now, conflicts occur. World prosperity or group prosperity? The lines have blurred, concurrent with the increasingly younger demographic changes of the group.

These days most of their time is spent protecting capitalist democracies from various terrorist factions around the world that would do harm to the world economy, as well as to protect the finances of the group, since they are closely tied together. Fanatical Islamic terrorists or communism - both of which are on the rise - cause global economic uncertainty. COMMON's investments are not unstable. Period.

The group has contacts and "moles" inside most governments around the world. No one knows to whom they are giving top-secret information. The moles are paid well and have been convinced they're doing the right thing for their own country. COMMON believes that all people, no matter what country or language spoken, are strikingly similar when it comes to patriotic dedication. If each mole can be convinced they are doing the right thing for their country, it's amazing what can be accomplished for the common good.

COMMON supplies sensitive and top-secret intelligence to select leaders who are in positions to authorize action. But the information provided is limited to what COMMON deems pertinent. With moles in every spy agency in the world, COMMON's staff sifts through the intelligence and marries the information together to predict future events. Then they share with the appropriate government only that information they feel will be beneficial to them.

Exactly what a government's response will be is left to that country's government, as long as the result favors COMMON's desired outcome. COMMON will nudge and persuade others, but never act themselves. Sometimes they witness a mission play-out live, but generally they enjoy their cozy cocoon in the French Alps and watch from a distance. Drones and satellite transmissions work well for that purpose.

Mr. Hill is a senior member of COMMON. He manipulates news stories to fit COMMON's needs. He is also the handler for the contact inside the United States. The U.S. is vital to COMMON since they are the lone world power and have the most powerful and sophisticated armed forces.

The group arranged for Isaac Jones to be assigned to the CIA and it was through their manipulation that he went on the Benghazi mission, the North Korean mission, and the Reagan mission, crippling key targets along the way. Unknown to them is the fact that Jones has just been taken. They've heard rumors about Jones being on a grab list, but decided he was a small pawn in their game and the target on his back was not vital to the interest of the group. They've felt that Jones, like many before him, is expendable, just another pawn on the chess board.

WASHINGTON, D.C.

Senator James Thurston is seated at his desk in his office on The Hill. It's pushing 7:00a.m. and his secretary hasn't yet arrived. He holds a cigar in one hand and a small tumbler of cognac in the other. His doctor told him to cut back on both, but not on mornings like this. He's been sitting staring at his phone for almost a half-hour trying to decide if he should make the call.

He finally picks up the phone and dials. It ticks him off to no end that when he asked a friend at the NSA to track the number he just dialed, he was told the number came back with no information. "It's a jumper," was the answer he got. A "jumper" is a secure phone line, whether analog or digital, that jumps its way around the world from phone hub to phone hub preventing its origin from being traced. He was told whoever had that number was serious about not being found. They provided an option to put a team on it to dig deeper. The Senator declined the offer since that could raise questions he didn't want to answer.

Thurston listened as the line rang three times. He was about to hang-up when the line connected, "Senator, this is an unexpected surprise," Mr. Hill says in his thick, Manchester accent.

Without hesitation Thurston burst out, "Isaac Jones has been grabbed!"

A long pause ensued, then, "I see," Hill replies, not overly excited.

"That's why I'm calling you. We don't know who...was it you?" The Senator's voice is intense.

"It wasn't us."

"Well, we're in a real crap-storm over here. They grabbed him out of a black location in the U.S. and I—"

Hill interrupts, "If they grabbed him out of a black location, you better check your house, Senator. It sounds unclean."

"What do you mean 'my house is unclean'?"

"You know what I mean. I will check into it, but I think you have a mole. And I know about moles."

The line goes dead in the Senator's ear. He slams the phone back into its carriage and takes a big gulp from his drink. Leaning back abruptly in his chair, looking at the crown molding above his head, he moans, "Good Lord!" to an empty ceiling in an empty office.

Chapter 6

The chopper carrying Deputy Director Waxman from Mountain Home Air Force Base lands in the center of the two streets adjacent the corner lot of Jones' townhouse. The sun is just starting to peep over the Mountains. It promises to be a beautiful day in the Northwest. The air is crisp without a cloud in the sky. Waxman had told Henry to lock the jet down until he returned.

The base supplied him a chopper and pilot. Half a dozen police cruisers with their red and blue lights flashing hold a perimeter, forbidding traffic from accessing the street and making safe for landing. The local police don't know exactly what is going on. They were simply told the Central Intelligence Agency was sending a VIP to the area, and they were to provide whatever was needed. All Waxman asked was to keep everyone out, including local law enforcement. He would take command of the scene upon his arrival.

AFB Military Police were also providing security; their presence reverberates in the neighborhood - men posted in full military gear on each point of the residence, with a dozen more lined-up on the street around the house making a human perimeter. Neighbors are peeking out of their windows, nervously watching the orderly activity. Waxman jumps down from the chopper onto the pavement. Eldon Chase meets him just outside of the rotor wash.

"It's been awhile, Eldon," Waxman greets, shaking his hand.

"I wish it was under better circumstances, Sir," he replies.

"So, what happened?"

"Lord knows. I woke from my sleep to a hellish noise. It sounded like a big crash coming from Isaac's house. I got up and looked out the back window. From my vantage, all I could see were flashlights and bursts of light. I grabbed my shotgun and went out the front door. I saw half a dozen men drag Isaac out of the house and put him in a black van. It was all precision teamwork, they were pros. I took a shot and had to take cover when they returned fire. They drove off, and I called it in. Who they are and how they found him is beyond me."

"Have you been inside?"

"Yes, for the most part it's clean. I found a few of these," Chase holds-out his hand, showing rubber bullets, "...and this," holding-up a syringe.

"Kinda messy, leaving those behind. Don't you think?"

"Well, it was a snatch and grab. You know how it goes, get in, get out, fast as possible. Besides, I don't think they were expecting me to show up." Eldon said with a slight smile.

Waxman nodded, "They drugged him?" Waxman asks.

"Whoever they are, they wanted him alive, Steven."

What is going on? Waxman wonders. "Alright, give me a walk-through," Waxman directs, as he heads toward the house.

FRENCH ALPS, FRANCE

In the Alps, the COMMON council of twelve is meeting.

"He said Jones was taken from a black location, and now they don't know where he is," Hill informs the group.

"We knew North Korea was aware of him months ago," said the blond woman with a thick Australian accent, seated to Hill's left.

"When we saw the communication between the American and North Korean we should have alerted our American contact," Hill comments.

"That is not in our interests. You know this. We do not get involved in affairs that don't directly coincide with our needs," said an overweight, balding man with a Bavarian accent seated across form Hill.

"Isaac Jones doesn't qualify as being in our interests? I disagree, no offence intended, my friend. The man handled three of our most ambitious issues of late. He's the American's point man on covert operations. Do we not owe him something?" Hill states clearly and simply.

"No, we do not," the heavy man answers. "We provide information to our contacts that benefit our organization. It is as simple as that. Everyone outside this group is replaceable, expendable. This is nothing new. We've seen it many times."

"I agree. But Isaac Jones is still a very vital asset to this group, and we should have protected him. To needlessly discard an asset is to squander it. Think about the big picture."

Sasha Brycekov, seated to Hill's left, has been watching this exchange intently. He is surprised how upset Mr. Hill is over Jones being taken, and decided to see if he can calm things down. "We do not even know if the North Koreans are the ones who have Jones. I suggest we reach out to our contacts and see what we can learn, then make a decision as to how, or if, we get involved," he adds to the discussion, in his thick Russian accent.

Some of the members nod in agreement. The division within the group is becoming more obvious.

An Asian man named Park, seated at the head of the table, says with authority, "I agree with Mr. Brycekov. Let us see what we can find out and take it up again in the morning. Mr. Hill, is that satisfactory?" he asks, not leaving any room for disagreement.

"It is," Mr. Hill answers, "but I'm not content with this option."

The meeting ends and Brycekov exits the conference room. He walks down the long hall to his quarters, and enters his office. After locking the door behind him, he curses out loud in Russian, reaching for his satellite phone. He sits in the chair at his desk and pivots around to his right, looking out the glass walls to see if anyone is approaching.

He's engaged in a very dangerous game. He has broken the most sacred rule of COMMON: *Never use the group's intelligence for personal gain.* The penalty for such an action is death.

The proof of the pudding, they say, is in the eating. It's been more than a saying in the COMMON world. In 2000, Alexander Litvinenko, a 43 year-old former Russian Federal Security Service agent (successor to the Russian KGB) had fled Russia to Britain, becoming a British citizen. He was loudly critical of the Kremlin and President Putin. He was also a member of COMMON.

After the Cold War, he found that being a Russian spy was not what it used to be. The pay was in the unstable rubles, and the benefits were even worse. He used intelligence COMMON had acquired, selling it to a British MI6 agent for almost a million pounds sterling. His plan was to disappear. One November evening in 2006, Litvinenko became ill after drinking some tea in a restaurant in London. He died three weeks later from an unhealthy ingestion of radioactive polonium-210. There were suspicions that the Russians killed him, as was the plan, but high-ups at COMMON knew the truth. COMMON contracted with two other former Russian spies to take him out for the simple act of using COMMON intelligence for personal gain.

Litvinenko was the most recent member to be eliminated by COMMON under a shadow of clandestineness, but other names are widely suspected, like President Kennedy, Senator Kennedy, Malcolm X, Franz Ferdinand, Former U.S. President Bill Clinton's Commerce Secretary, Ron Brown, Former U.S. President Harry Truman's Secretary of

Defense, James Forrestal, and even U.S. Army General George S. Patton. Some say Patton used intelligence provided by COMMON as the Third Army made its way through Europe. All died untimely deaths under incredibly suspicious...and well-planned...circumstances.

Sasha Brycekov has been using COMMON intelligence to his advantage outside of the group's approval for years. He knows it's a dangerous game he's playing, but his ego is stronger than his logic. He's a forgettable, average looking man who knows how to blend in, a trait he learned from being a former Russian spy himself.

Brycekov's sandy hair seems to always need trimming on his brow. His tall, slender body contrasts his very puffy Russian-looking facial features. His COMMON predecessor was a former KGB who sponsored and mentored him for twenty years. Brycekov was eager to take his seat upon his passing.

He believes in COMMON's mission, and not so secretly desires his homeland to return to its previous Communist glory. Brycekov feared for his country while George W. Bush was President. *This cowboy is an insane war-monger*, he thought, with no doubt that if Russia presented a threat to the U.S., Bush would hit his country relentlessly, in whatever fashion possible, outside of using nukes, of course.

When Barack Obama became President, Brycekov relaxed. COMMON helped fund the tall, slender, chain-smoking Chicago community activist's billion dollar presidential election runs. Their thought was that Obama would level the world playing field a bit, knocking-down America's stance as a world power more than a notch or two. They knew Obama was more interested in a world balance of power than American dominance. And they were accurate. They invested against American interests and made a fortune in China, while helping fund Russia's annexation of Crimea.

Once Brycekov saw that Obama was going to do nothing about Crimea, and ignored the "line in the sand" drawn with regard to Syria, he knew it was finally the right time to send a message to the United States, that they were no longer the Big Dog, and Russia was coming back. President Putin, also former KGB, understood, just as Brycekov did, that the U.S. needed a reality check. Not long ago, Brycekov recruited his boyhood friend Nicola Poloski, to team-up with some very dangerous Islamist terrorists to send the message to the United States.

That's when Isaac Jones got under his skin and became his Target Number One.

Chapter 7

Brycekov, without COMMON's approval, recruited Nicola Poloski to strike at America's pride by initiating acts of terror at significant historical locations around the globe – locations that honor the Presidency of Ronald Reagan. Poloski hired some former KGB agents and teamed-up with fanatical Islamic Muslim terrorists to carry out their plans, including the senseless murders of American citizens on American soil in significant cities of Reagan's life. In a brazen act of mocking the former President, the murderers scattered pictures of Reagan next to the bodies. Then they bombed an airport in Granada, the site of a military success for Reagan in 1983, a bold military initiative which led to the first-ever free elections in Granada. They also bombed a Reagan statue in Hungary, and attempted to bomb The Brandenburg Gate in Berlin, where Reagan gave his famous "Tear Down this Wall" speech in 1987. Their final plan was to level the London residence of former British Prime Minister Thatcher, but Isaac Jones led the efforts against them, and their mission failed.

In Germany, Jones saved an eleven-year-old boy from martyring himself with a suicide vest that would have destroyed The Brandenburg Gate. Jones and his men also killed Brycekov's band of terrorists attempting to destroy the Thatcher residence, including Poloski. Brycekov tried to disrupt Jones' plans, but COMMON intervened, deciding it was not in the group's best interest.

They knew President Obama would be forced to respond, despite how passive he was on foreign affairs. Ironically, COMMON didn't know that one of their own was behind the incident.

Brycekov was furious about the failed plan that he initiated. He started monitoring American communications. As a result, he discovered that assistant CIA Director, Trent McBride, was acting erratically, trying to second-guess Isaac Jones' actions. It was becoming an obsession of sorts, and McBride was certain Jones had been dispatched covertly around the world by the CIA – but couldn't prove it.

As a result, Brycekov made a bold move. He reached out to McBride. Brycekov knew the North Korean government was seething about their missile and drone center being bombed, suspecting it was an American operation. Brycekov also discovered that McBride, too, had suspicions of the CIA's involvement in the North Korean mission, which occurred without his approval, and was intent on proving it.

Brycekov, enraged with anger, focused on one thing; getting rid of the man who foiled his Reagan terror plot and killed his friend and comrade; Isaac Jones had to be taken care of.

BOISE, IDAHO

Waxman and Eldon walk through Isaac Jones' house. In the living room, everything is disheveled; furniture knocked over and broken glass.

"Wow," Waxman sighs, his phone rings, and looking at the screen he sees "POTUS Chief of Staff, Harrison."

"Great," he says out loud, shaking his head. The last thing he wanted was the White House getting wind of the problem and start asking questions. "Hello?"

"Steven, its Gio Harrison, how are you?"

"Ah, well it's been a busy morning. How are you, Sir?"

"I'm great. I won't keep you, I know you're a busy man. Listen, the President and I would like to sit down with you. Nothing formal, just a short chat. Can you fit us in?", he asks with a chuckle, knowing that asking someone to "fit the President of the United States into their schedule" is coyly beyond rhetorical.

"Sure, of course, Sir. When?"

"The sooner the better, today?" Harrison asks.

"Well, that might be difficult. I'm out in the field. I'm..." he pauses not wanting to open the door for questions about where he is and why. Although, *It is the President's Chief of Staff*, he thinks to himself. "I'm in Idaho dealing with a small issue right now, Sir."

"Idaho? Is everything alright, Steven?"

Deciding to not get off on the wrong foot with the new administration, he reluctantly opens up the hornets' nest. "Well, to be honest, we do have an issue. One of our covert assets appears to have been taken out of a black location."

"What?"

"I'm on location with the house guardian now. May I call you back when I know more?"

"I'd say you better call me back. Who's the missing asset?"

"Sir?"

"Who's the asset?" Harrison asks again, irritated he has to repeat his question.

"Sir, I don't know if that's—"

Rudely interrupting, Harrison demands, "Mr. Waxman, who's the asset?"

"Isaac Jones."

"I don't know the name. Who's the guardian?"

"Eldon Chase."

"Get done what needs done there, then you and Chase get to the White House as soon as you can. I'll adjust the President's schedule as necessary."

"Sir, Chase is a retired agent who—"

"I know who Chase is. I want him with you when you brief the President, Steven."

"No offense, Sir, but do you really think this rises to the level of a White House briefing?" Waxman said trying to deflate the issue.

"I guess we'll find out, won't we"

"Yes, Sir. One more thing…"

"Yes?"

"Jones is, well, he's more than a black operative, Sir. He's been off the books for most of his time here. If you could keep this…"

"I understand. I won't mention it to anyone but the President. It will stay between us until the President decides who, if anyone, needs to be brought in."

"Thank you, Sir."

"Get back to Washington as soon as you can."

The call goes dead. Waxman looks at Eldon who had been listening to one side of the conversation. "Looks like you're coming with me."

"Where?"

"To the White House."

Chapter 8

Deputy Director Waxman's executive assistant, Ms. Stella, is at her desk trying to find busy work to keep her mind off Jones being missing. She's daydreaming, really. Thinking about happier things trying to stay positive. She remembers delivering take-out Chinese food to Jones' house the night little Michael was accepted to his new school. It was a celebration. Michael would be going to the same school as his father. They all ate together at Jones' dinner table with smiles all around. She smiled at the memory. Then, something on her computer monitor caught her eye that made her heart beat faster. It was an urgent information flash from South Korea, stating that during the previous night a South Korean agent had been kidnapped and is missing in action. The asset's name: Yon U. Stella knew Yon helped Jones during the North Korean mission and she even met Yon once a while back when she was in the States visiting Jones and Michael. "Oh, Bugger!" she said, shaking her head, while reaching for her phone.

Waxman and Eldon are in-flight back to Washington, D.C. when Waxman's phone rings. "Hi, Stella."

"I think we have a real problem," she informs him.

"Tell me something I don't know," he says with an edge, out of character for him. The stress of Jones' abduction, and now the White House breathing down his neck, it's all now getting the better of him.

"I just saw a flash from South Korea. Yon U is missing, presumed to have been kidnapped."

"What?!" Waxman abruptly replies.

"It just came over the wire. This can't be a bloody coincidence."

"No, it can't. Find-out as much as you can. Make contact with the South Koreans and let them know about Jones, but tell them not to share that information with anyone."

"Yes, Sir! I'll meet you on the tarmac when you land," she says.

"I'll be going directly from the airport to the White House. Make sure the driver is informed. And I don't want anyone knowing about it, understand?"

"The White House? Will do. Anything else?" she asks.

"Just set it up, I'll fill you in later. Don't tell McBride... or Thurston or Lopez."

"Ok. I'll see you soon."

"Stella, make sure the South Koreans keep their mouths shut."

"I will." She hangs-up, lost deep in thought. *I can't just sit here.* Then an idea comes to her, and she considers the possible consequences of taking action without approval. After a few minutes of figuring out some details, she decides she is willing to take any heat that might come of her actions. She picks up her phone and dials. After a few rings, a man answers, "Warren speaking."

"Mr. Warren, this is Stella from Deputy Director Waxman's office in Washington."

Elliot Warren is Isaac Jones' best friend, and frequently helps him on missions when the British government allows it. Warren is a ten-year member of the British Secret Intelligence Service (SIS). Before that, he served in Her Majesty's army and did two tours in Iraq and Afghanistan.

Not long ago, as an Army Ranger, Jones met Warren during a joint covert operation, and the two warriors have been pals ever since. Being all muscle and no fluff, Warren is not the stereotype, which most Americans think of Brits. He prefers a dark beer rather than afternoon tea, and has an Old Hollywood "Steve-McQueen-cool" about him. He's calm and confident, sometimes even a bit overconfident, which appeals to Jones. He has sandy blond hair and blue eyes. He has a slightly-too-large nose that reminds new acquaintances of a bird's beak – but only when they first meet him. Warren's sense of humor is a great balance to Jones' seriousness. Not that Warren can't be serious, when he's working, he's all business. But, when he's off-the-clock, his sense of very-British humor is on full display.

"Oh, Ms. Stella! I know who you are, Jonesy's told me all about you. To what do I owe this pleasure, my dear? And please, call me Elliot."

Stella smiles, hearing that Jones had told him about her. "Elliot, we have a real problem here. Deputy Director

Waxman doesn't know I'm calling you, but I think you should know what's happening."

Warren can clearly hear the worry in Stella's voice. "Alright, birdy. What's happened? What's wrong?"

"Isaac is missing. He was grabbed out of his black location."

"Whoa, slow down! What are you talking about? When? By whom? Are you sure?"

Stella informs Warren everything she knows, in detail. Her hope is that an agent of Warren's talent might provide some insight, which they hadn't thought of.

"Bloody hell! Waxman is on his way back to D.C. now?" he asks.

"Yes."

"I'm on my way from London. Call me if you get any more information. Tell Waxman I want in on this and I'm not bloody asking. I'll call you from the air with my arrival time. Have a car pick me up, got it?"

"Yes, Elliot. Thank you. Hurry!"

"Calm down, Darlin'. Jonesy is a tough chap, and he's smart. We'll get him back. Count on it."

Warren hangs-up and looks at his watch, just after 1:00 p.m. He heads to a closet, grabbing his go-bag, and is out the door and en route to the airport in less than five minutes. *Hang on, ol' buddy. I'm coming!*

Chapter 9

Assistant CIA Director, Trent McBride, arrived later than usual to his office. As they say in the cloakrooms of Congress, as well as in the overblown, ego-driven coffee shops of the entertainment industry, he *"took an early meeting"* at a downtown coffee shop with Senator Theresa Heart of Tennessee. Senator Heart sits on the Senate Intelligence Committee, an odd place for someone who believes the CIA needs to be reeled-in. It's a Democratic Party mantra that never wants to end. She recommended to the President that McBride be nominated as the new CIA Director. Although she doesn't really care that much for McBride, she knows he can be managed by her committee. A while back, she and McBride attempted to blindside Waxman during a budget hearing. McBride told the Senator he thought Waxman had sent a deep-cover asset on unsanctioned missions. When she went after Waxman during the hearing, Senator Thurston got in the way, blocking all of her questions. Waxman was never forced to answer her inquiry. Although McBride can't prove it, he believes Waxman sent a new asset on these unsanctioned missions and he's shared his theory with the Senator. The agent? Isaac Jones.

Heart has an unrealistic opinion about the level influence she exerts with President Mitchell, believing she wields more power than she actually does. As it is with many career politicians that have watched the revolving door of the Oval Office, Senator Heart buys into her own overinflated ego, thinking, *President's come and go. It's we who live our lives on The Hill who run this town.*

She believes President Mitchell will agree with her recommendation for McBride to run the CIA. *Hell, he can't even recognize when I'm manipulating him*, she often boasts over lunch with her lover and Chief of Staff, Paula St. George.

She's dead wrong. The President and Heart are on very different sides of the aisle. He thinks she's far too full of herself and needs a reality check. She thinks he's a political adolescent without the wherewithal to understand key strategies.

The President thinks that ignoring her recommendation of McBride might just be the signal she needs to understand that her party is no longer calling the shots. President Mitchell also believes that Trent McBride is already in over his head as Assistant CIA Director, and would never be able to manage the entire Agency. The President has already determined that he will not nominate McBride.

Arriving at the coffee shop for his early meeting with Heart and St. George, McBride hears Frank Sinatra's "Come Fly with Me" playing in the background, perfectly setting the mood for the conversation they are about to have.

> *"Once I get you up there*
> *where the air is rarified,*
> *we'll just glide, starry-eyed..."*

"Once you're confirmed as Director, we have a lot of work to do, Mr. McBride."

"Thanks for the confidence, Senator, but I haven't even been nominated yet." McBride smiled as he took a sip of his coffee, thinking to himself, *'CIA Director McBride' sounds pretty good! All my work is finally about to pay-off.*

"Oh, don't you worry. I personally recommended you to the President," she responds confidently while looking over at Ms. St. George.

"That's right," St. George adds. "When Senator Heart pushes an issue, Washington, D.C. feels the pressure...especially down at Pennsylvania Avenue."

"I appreciate your faith in me, both of you," he thanks them.

"I have faith in your ability to do the job, but I also need to have faith that you will clean house, as well. There needs to be some real changes. We can't just go around the world using our military and interfering in other countries' business, that is, unless we're bringing our transformational culture to them. I'm not pushing you on the President to continue promoting the status quo. No, we need transformative change that creates a new status quo. Simply put, the Agency needs an enema, and I'm counting on you," Senator Heart states.

"This conversation has been going on for decades in this town, but it never seems to change. I'll do my best, but some of the old guard will give me resistance. They might have to go, and that will cause a lot of angst around town," McBride responds.

Heart looks up from sipping her coffee. "You're talking about Waxman?"

"I am. He will have to go if we want to make any real changes. Getting rid of Steven Waxman will be a big first step in the right direction. His old school ways represent all that's wrong with the CIA. He's cut from the same cloth as Christensen, and we both know what a miserable and dangerous Director he was," McBride says.

Heart sets her cup of coffee on the table, glancing casually at McBride, then over to her Chief of Staff, then around the room. "Be careful what you say out loud, Trent. Christensen is still a very powerful man. You wouldn't want him to know you felt that way." She pauses and whispers, "Not that I disagree." St. George nods in agreement.

"Waxman will be the first to go and then we take control of all our covert operatives. I think the entire black program needs to be shut down, or at least significantly limited."

Senator Heart smiles. "I agree."

The meeting ends with McBride walking on air as he strides down the long hallway to his office in the CIA headquarters. *The future is bright, so bright I gotta' wear shades*, he smiles to himself, thinking of a song he remembered from years ago. As McBride approaches his office, he sees his secretary, Hillary, stand up from her desk with wide eyes. "Good Morning, Hillary. What's going on?"

"Where have you been?" she asks.

McBride's facial response clearly indicates that she had better be careful talking to him that way.

"I need to speak with you, in your office," she says just above a whisper, but with urgency.

McBride walks into his office with Hillary right on his heels. Now, behind closed doors, he sits at his desk with Hillary standing directly in front of him. "So?"

All she says is, "Isaac Jones."

"What about him?"

"You have to keep quiet about it because it's above Top Secret, and I'm not supposed to know," Hillary cautions.

"What's above Top Secret?"

"Apparently, Jones was grabbed out of the Idaho black location last night."

"What?!" McBride slumps down in his chair. "Tell me everything you know."

Hillary has been McBride's secretary the entire time he's been at the Agency, but she's been working in the office for over 30 years. Over time, she's learned which other secretaries are "in-the-know" and which ones are willing to gossip about it. After arriving this morning, while getting her morning coffee down in the Agency café, she got an earful from some of the loose lips she's grown to value. When Isaac Jones' name came up, she knew McBride would want to know about it. It's not that she has any personal allegiance to McBride, but she's learned how to make herself invaluable, almost irreplaceable, to each of her bosses. It's called "job security."

Hillary informs McBride about Jones being taken, and Eldon Chase attempting to intervene. Further, she explains that Waxman flew to the location and is now in-flight returning with Chase. Also, that a female agent from South Korea had been grabbed and it is assumed the two incidents are somehow related. Then she the drops the bomb: Waxman is scheduled to go from the airport directly to the White House to personally brief President Mitchell.

McBride looks at her with a dull, but focused, stare. He isn't surprised Hillary had obtained this information. He's always known she has a particular edge to her – almost as though she were a field agent inside the Agency. He found out early-on how lucky he was to have a seasoned assistant who knew how to extract Intel from the other assistants. Hillary informs him she got her morning scoop from a secretary who works in the office next to Waxman's, and she overheard Stella talking about it to someone.

A worried look comes over McBride's face, but not because he is worried about Jones. Something else is troubling him. It's as if he isn't surprised about WHAT happened, but is surprised that it DID happen. "Who's this 'Eldon Chase'?" he asks.

"He's the black location guardian."

"'Black location guardian'? I didn't know there was such a thing."

"Yes, all black locations have a guardian to keep an eye on the location while the asset is away. They're also tasked with keeping tabs on the mental health of the asset."

"I guess that makes sense," he says. *I probably should have known that*, he thinks.

ABOVE WASHINGTON, D.C.

Henry informs Waxman and Eldon they are on final approach and will soon be landing in Washington, D.C.

"Sorry you had to come along, Eldon. I'm not sure why the President wanted you to come."

"It's probably because I know the President," he replies.

"You know President Mitchell?"

"Yes, I met him when he was still a Senator. Right after I retired from the field, I worked his security detail for the Secret Service, then became a black location guardian."

"I didn't know that." Waxman's phone rings. He looks at the screen, "Crap, it's McBride." He answers, "Hello?"

"Steven, I just heard what happened to Jones. Why didn't you call me?"

"Sorry, things we're so crazy, I forgot."

"You forgot. You didn't think that your boss should know one of our assets was grabbed?"

"Listen, Trent, I said it's been a crazy morning. One of MY assets has been grabbed out of what was supposed to be a black location. I've been kind of busy and I really don't need you on my ass right now," Waxman snaps.

Waxman and McBride have never gotten along well. Never. Waxman is everything McBride isn't. Unlike McBride, Waxman has the respect of the people who work at the

Agency, up and down the ladder, and he has worked his way up the chain of command, earning every promotion through hard work and personal sacrifice. For Waxman, the Agency IS his life. Everything else comes second...everything.

Since McBride is much the opposite of Waxman, they bump heads more than they get along. Waxman is the Deputy Director of the CIA's National Clandestine Service. Trent McBride, however, is the Assistant Director of the CIA. He's the number two man in the Agency, hired to work directly under the Director. Now that the Director has retired, McBride has taken it upon himself to assume some of the duties, as if he's already been confirmed as the new Director.

However, McBride is resented by most of the CIA staff. He didn't work his way up the chain of command, like Waxman; he was brought in from the outside as a political appointee. He treats employees, even those who have more working knowledge and experience than him, as underlings, and presents himself as knowing more than they do about national security.

On the phone call, McBride can tell Waxman is in a foul mood. He decided to change the subject to the real reason for his call: the White House. Deep down, he is seething at the idea of Waxman briefing the President personally. *Waxman works for me, I should be the one going to the White House*, he argues to himself. "I hear you're going to the White House as soon as you land. Why don't you swing by and pick me up on your way. I'd like to hear your brief, too."

"Not going to happen, Trent. I have specific orders to go directly to the White House when I land."

"Steven, you work for me. I give you your orders," McBride presses.

"Yes, I do work for you, and you work for the President. So, if you want to be at the meeting, drive yourself. Goodbye."

McBride hears the line go dead and curses. "I can't wait to see his face the day I become Director and fire his ass!" he says out loud to an empty room. He pushes a button on his phone and Hillary answers.

"Hillary, get me the President's Chief of Staff on the line."

After a few minutes Chief of Staff Harrison answers. "I'm having a crazy morning, Trent. What can I do for you?"

"Good morning, Sir. I hear you're having Steven Waxman come to see the President this morning. I thought I'd tag along, if it's alright."

"I appreciate the offer, Trent, but I think we've got it covered. Anything else?"

McBride was at a loss for words. He didn't expect the cold reception. "Um, well you know Waxman works directly under me, and since I haven't gotten a full briefing yet I thought we could kill two birds with one stone."

"Give it a rest, Trent. You're not fooling me. You want face time with the President, hoping it helps your chances at the Director's chair. Today is not a day for political posturing. If you want a briefing on this mess, get it on your own time, after Waxman briefs the President. Anything else?"

"No, Sir. Thank you." McBride hangs up and slumps back in his chair. Knowing the call didn't go well, he decides he needs to get his arms around the situation by making a phone call, but not inside the office. He opens his desk drawer and grabs an encrypted satellite phone. He steps out of the office door telling Hillary, "I'll be back later. Call me if you get any more information."

Sitting at her desk, Hillary finds meaningless things to do for about ten minutes, to make sure her boss isn't coming right back. Looking around and not seeing anyone paying attention to her, she grabs her personal iPhone from her purse. She scrolls through her contacts, finding the one she's looking for, and presses the call button. After two rings, the familiar voice of the former CIA Director Christensen answers with a simple "Hello."

"He's gone out," she informs.

"Thank you, Hillary. Let's have dinner soon. You and your bottom-of-the-pond-sucking, political-consultant-for-the-wrong-team, husband of yours, ok?"

"Ha! You grumpy ol' coot. I'll ask him," she replies.

"I may be grumpy…but old? My dear, I'm just hitting my prime."

Hillary giggles, "Goodbye, Mr. Director."

Christensen hangs-up and logs into his encrypted email account on his computer. Finding the address he's looking for, he types five words, and clicks "Send."

In the French Alps, Mr. Hill is sitting at his desk when he receives the email from Christensen. It reads: "He just left the office."

He replies with a "Thank you" message, and then deletes it.

Hill looks through the glass walls of his office. Across the hall from him, Brycekov is also seated at a desk. "the cats away, let's see what game the mice play," he whispers out loud to no one in particular.

Chapter 10

VALDEZ, ALASKA

Isaac Jones is awakened by the tremendously harsh thud of landing gear touching down on the rough tarmac of a small, semi-deserted, airport on the outskirts of Valdez, Alaska. He pretends to still be unconscious. The men quickly gather their gear, speaking harshly. Jones doesn't understand their words, but he immediately recognizes them...Korean.

Three men lift Jones up, two by the arms and one grabbing his legs, and carry him down the stairs to a van waiting on the tarmac. The crisp, cool air helps clear his head. It smells like the sea. He also feels the sun's heat on his face and closed eyelids. The mixture of the two senses feels good. They quickly load-up in the van and drive out of the airport. Jones is in the very back of the van, on the floor, still bound at his wrists and ankles. The driver slips the van down an embankment, the windows are cracked open and the smell of the salty sea air increases in Jones' lungs, and his head becomes clearer.

Koreans? How did they find me? How did they know I was in North Korea? It should have made perfect sense that the Koreans would be after Yon and him, since they were both responsible for the destruction of the North Korean missile and drone control center. *But…how did they figure-out where I've been hiding away?* He silently wonders. *I've got to get my hands unbound and activate my tracker*, pulling at the plastic cuffs around his wrists, but with no progress.

The van comes to an abrupt stop and the men get out. Jones lifts his head and looks around to confirm he's alone in the van. He pushes his chin into his chest allowing the chain around his neck holding the St. Michael pendant to catch tightly around the bottom edge of his chin. He forcefully pushes his chin upward snapping the light gold chain. The necklace and pendant fall to the floor.

First, the men unload their gear and then three men come back and grab Jones. As they pull him out, he opens one eye seeing an extremely large, black cargo ship with a red stripe sitting in harbor on an endless body of water. Jones hears one of the men say something he doesn't understand, but the men carrying him stop. As a man approaches, Jones squeezes his eyes shut. He feels the now-familiar sting to his neck and then burning under the skin of his face, his mouth goes dry, and the world goes dark again. His last thought before he blacks out is, *these guys are really starting to piss me off!*

WASHINGTON, D.C.

A black Chevrolet Suburban is waiting on the tarmac when the CIA jet lands. Deputy Director Waxman and Eldon Chase deplane and hop in. They are quickly on their way to the White House. Stella is seated in the front passenger seat. She hands Waxman a black CIA folder with the alert from South Korea about Yon U.

Waxman peruses it briefly and looks up, "Tell me about Jones, Eldon. You've been watching him for some time now. What's your impression?"

"Isaac Jones is a complicated man. He's fit - when he's home, he goes running almost every day. I'm not sure how far, but he's usually gone an hour or so. He doesn't talk much. When I've asked him about his job, he keeps the conversation pretty vague, which isn't surprising for a man who isn't supposed to tell people what he does for a living. He seems healthy, mentally and physically. The only thing..." Chase pauses as if in thought.

"What?" Waxman presses.

"He seems to be at the beginning stages of what I would call a spiritual quest."

Waxman shakes his head, "What does *that* mean?"

"As you know, outside my official CIA duties, I pastor at a small community church. I've used this position as my cover story," he smiles. "It's always much easier to make a solid cover if parts of it are true, and my faith is the truest part of my life. After telling Isaac I was a pastor, much of our conversations have centered on faith issues, and questions he has about that. He seems to thirst for knowledge, and an affirmation that the Lord doesn't frown on him for tasks his country asks him to do."

"Really?" Waxman seems surprised. "What do you tell him?"

"Interesting you should ask. I remember vividly my last conversation with him. I tried to give him inspiration from both the Psalms and the Book of John:

> *"Blessed be the Lord, my Rock, who trains my hand for war, and my fingers for battle";* and
> *"Greater love has no one than this, that he lay down his life for his friends."*

Eldon takes a deep breath. "I wonder if any of Isaac's friends will give that much to try and get him back home," he looks thoughtfully at Waxman, who seems rapt in the soulful moment.

Stella's eyes fill with tears. She doesn't turn around in her seat to look at Eldon, but instead continues looking out the front window, concealing her emotions. Part of her own frustrations are her emotions about Jones being missing. Over the years, she has seen many assets disappear, presumed dead or captured. It's the reality of her job. But for some reason, this Jones-grab is hitting her deeper than others.

"You've grown to really like him, haven't you?" Waxman inquires of Chase.

"Yes, I care for him a great deal, and respect him. He has a good heart, Steven. He's given much for his country. We can't leave him behind. He wouldn't leave you or me behind."

"We're going to get him home. I promise you that," Waxman affirms. He looks out his side window…staring back at him is the front lawn of the White House. "Now I have to make the President see how important he is."

Chapter 11

Trent McBride is traveling south in his black Cadillac CTS, away from the CIA headquarters in Langley. It's a smooth riding vehicle; McBride always wanted a Cadillac. When he took the job as Assistant Director of the CIA, he was able to choose any vehicle he wanted, regardless of the cost, so he chose his dream car, without any concern that it would be paid for by the American taxpayers. He isn't traveling to any particular destination, just driving in circles. He needs to make a call, but not on the Agency phone in his office. He knows all lines inside the building are monitored by software developed by the NSA, scanning for keywords and voice recognition, looking for double agents inside the agency. McBride isn't a double agent, but this call would raise all kinds of alarms. Questions would be asked that he did not want to answer.

He loves his country, but adamantly disagrees with the direction the Agency has been going.

In particular, he has concerns with what he believes are unofficial missions Isaac Jones has engaged in. He's failed numerous times to get Jones under control. He's tried to put pressure on Deputy Director Waxman, demanding an explanation of what exactly Jones does at the CIA, but Waxman continues to deflect. McBride was getting extremely frustrated, until a few months ago when something happened. He received an anonymous, encrypted email on his personal account. Even now, he doesn't know how the person got his private email address. The message simply stated, "Your suspicions about Isaac Jones are correct. We can help you take control of the situation." He must have read the simple, two-sentence message a dozen times trying to decide if it was a joke, trap, or legit. Hesitantly, he responded with a short reply, "You have my attention." When he didn't received a response for two days he started to panic, thinking it was indeed a trap. But on the evening of the third day it came: "If I give you the information you seek, there is no going back. Understand?" McBride replied, "Understood."

Another three days went by without any response. That evening, upon returning home from the office, there was a package sitting on his front step. He picked it up, noticing it didn't have any postage markings, just simply his name. He looked around the neighborhood to see if perhaps it was a trap. Not seeing any surveillance vehicles, he took the package inside the garage. He placed the package on his worktable and stood looking at it. Everything inside him screamed, "DON'T OPEN IT!" But he gave-in to curiosity, driven by his disdain for Jones, and cut open the box. Inside was an encrypted satellite phone with a note stating, "One number is programmed into this phone. If you make the call there is no going back. It's your decision, Mr. McBride."

He closed his eyes. *It could be a trap*, his mind cautioned again. *Then again, it might be everything I need to expose Jones.* He took the phone, and went into the back of his house, to the living room bar cabinet and poured himself a tumbler of vodka. He belted down the drink, then pushed the call button.

Even though that was months ago, McBride can still hear the voice in his head as clear as though it was yesterday, saying, "Hello, Mr. McBride. I've been expecting your call." The voice sounded like a male, but was electronically enhanced to mask the identity. It reminded him of the kind of voice often heard on an undercover news story where the whistle-blower's face is blacked out and the voice is altered to protect the person's identity.

"You said you had information for me?" McBride choked as he said the words.

"I do. But, if I give you the information you desire, I'll need a favor in return, no questions asked. However, I think you will find this little arrangement mutually beneficial to us both," the voice said. McBride thought he caught a slight accent, but couldn't make it out.

"That depends on what you want and what you're giving."

"I need your assurance that if I give you the information, you will do for me the favor I need."

"I will not commit treason to my country, let's get that out on the table right now," McBride stated.

"Treason? I wouldn't think of asking that, of you," the voice said.

"Then, what?"

"Just an address," the voice said calmly.

A curious look came over McBride's face, "An address? Whose?"

"We will get to that in due time. Do we have a deal?"

McBride closed his eyes again and paused, as though weighing the risks, "Okay…we have a deal," McBride responded. Giving out an address isn't that big of a deal, he decided; saving our nation IS.

"Fine. Your suspicions about Isaac Jones are correct."

"What suspicions are you referring to?" McBride said, fishing for more.

"Jones, along with a team he put together, killed those men in Iran. He also was partly responsible for the destruction of the missile and drone command center in North Korea."

"Oh, come on, I've suspected that for months," McBride said, as if the man was now wasting his time. "Can you prove it?"

"Yes."

"How?"

"Look at the screen on the phone," the voice instructed.

McBride pulled the phone away from his ear and looked at the screen. Two pictures appeared. The first one was dark and distant. By using his fingers on the screen he zoomed in on what looked like men exiting a shack. The shack could be in the Middle East, but was not distinct. He zoomed in on the faces of the men. There were three men carrying another man who looked to be injured. A fourth man followed behind; McBride looked more closely…it was Isaac Jones!

"You have my attention," he said, putting the phone back to his ear.

"That was in Iran. Now, look again."

McBride again looked at the screen. A new photo displayed. It showed two people on an old-style BMW R75 motorcycle, like what the Germans rode in WWII. They were driving by what looked like a waterfront. He zoomed in on the faces. In the carriage was an Asian female, who was holding a rifle. McBride didn't recognize her, but the driver was unmistakable...Isaac Jones. The image then disappeared from the screen. He put the phone back to his ear.

"North Korea?" he asked.

"Yes."

"Who's the female?"

"She's of no concern to you, but she assisted Jones in the mission," the voice stated.

"I need those images back. I can take them to Senator Heart. We could have a Senate oversight committee called in a couple of days and have Jones thrown in jail," McBride said.

"No, that is not our desired outcome."

"Not your desired outcome? Then, what is?

"I don't want you to do anything but provide me with an address."

"What address?" McBride asked.

"Isaac Jones' safe house."

"For what?" McBride was now concerned.

"Let's just say there are people who want to hold him accountable for his actions."

"I can hold him accountable in front of a United States Senate committee, and Waxman along with him."

"That's not how we want it, Mr. McBride. We have a deal."

"You can't grab a CIA asset out of a safe house here in America and think you can get away with it. I won't be a part of that. The heat from something like that would be extremely intense."

"You don't have to. All I need is the location, we'll handle the rest." The voice paused, "I thought you wanted to get rid of Jones and 'clean house' at the Agency? Isn't that what you told Senator Heart?"

"I don't give a damn about Isaac Jones. He's a criminal as far as I'm concerned. I care about my career being jeopardized in the process. I'm not an idiot!" Then the man's last comment dawned on McBride, "How do you know what I told Senator Heart? Do you have me under surveillance?" McBride began to panic inside.

"I told you there was no going back if you made this call," the voice warned.

"I haven't done anything!" McBride yelled.

The next thing McBride heard made his face go white. His own voice speak back to him:

"Getting rid of Steven Waxman will be a big first step in the right direction. His old school ways represent all that's wrong with the CIA. He's cut from the same cloth as Christensen, and we both know what a miserable and dangerous Director he was."

Then he heard Senator Heart's voice:

"Be careful what you say out loud, Trent. Christensen is still a very powerful man. You wouldn't want him to know you felt that way."

There was a click, and he heard his voice from just a few minutes ago:

"Okay…we have a deal."
"Fine. Your suspicions about Isaac Jones are correct."
"What suspicions are you referring to?"

"That doesn't mean I told you anything," he blurted out, knowing now that this conversation was being recorded.

"No, but if I should send this to Mr. Waxman, telling him you were plotting against the Agency, how do you think he will respond? Probably not good for you. As a matter of fact, I would suspect a Senate hearing would take place, just like you suggested, but you would be the star," the voice said.

McBride slammed his fist on the table in front of him with anger, "Fine, I'll get you the address. But, then I'm out of it. And, I suggest you wait a few months until I'm confirmed as the new Director. I'll be in a better position to provide cover," said McBride, trying to get control of the deal, but the line went dead.

Later that day, per the terms of the deal, McBride sent a text from the satellite phone of Jones' safe house location in Idaho.

Now, driving aimlessly around the beltway of D.C., considering what Hillary just told him, McBride realized the man obviously didn't take his suggestion of waiting until he was appointed Director. McBride picks-up the satellite phone in his car and hits the call button. After a few rings, the same man's voice answers.

"Mr. McBride, I wasn't expecting this call," the voice said through the same electronic voice changer.

"I thought you were going to wait until I was confirmed as Director."

Chapter 12

After delivering Waxman and Chase to the White House, Ms. Stella returned to her office at the CIA headquarters. She offered to wait, but Deputy Waxman told her it wasn't necessary – and the glances by the Secret Service personnel supported that sentiment. She now sits at her desk, nervously waiting for any news. She looks around the office and for the first time in all the years she's worked there, she notices how cold the building looks and feels. There's a framed picture of the new President on the wall and a small black sofa just to her left, where visitors wait to see her boss. But other than that, it's a bare, and almost bone-chilling, atmosphere. *Perhaps it's time to go home and get out of this retched business. I miss London. I miss my friends*, she thinks. Being an only child, she's alone now. Her mother and father had her late in life, so they were new parents when their friends were becoming grandparents. They were always supportive and patient with her as a child. It was during her first year at college in America that her father passed away in his sleep, and shortly after that, her mother followed. She misses them dearly. Her iPod was shuffling through her favorite songs. "Haunt Me" by Sade came on.

> *"So should you ever doubt me*
> *If it's help that you need*

Never dare to doubt me."

Tears bubble up in her eyes as she thinks of Jones. "Bloody hell! Pull yourself together, missy!" she scolds herself out loud, wiping her eyes to make sure her mascara doesn't smudge. She reaches over and turns-off the music, taking a deep breath to help regain her composure. Her office phone rings, "Deputy Director Waxman's office," she answers.

"Stella, it's General Moony. Is he in?"

"No, Sir," she sits up in her chair. "He's at the White House. Did you find out anything?"

"Sorry, Ms. Stella, I don't know anything else yet. The staff is still checking. I'll get back to you when I get more information."

"Blast it!" she said louder than she meant.

"Stella, we're going to find him."

ABOVE WASHINGTON, D.C.

Flying high over Washington, D.C. a small drone is stealthily flying in a wide circle. The sky is clear and the white drone is almost invisible. The drone found its target and is now recording both video and audio of a black Cadillac CTS which seems to be driving in circles around the Beltway.

"I never said we were going to wait until you became Director before we moved on Jones," the voice informs McBride concisely. "Besides, I'm not as confident as you that you're going to be the next Director, although I would prefer that you were."

"What do you know? Do you have inside information on who the President is looking at?" he asks in a panic.

"No, no. Calm down. Just a gut feeling. I could be wrong."

"Who are you?" McBride asks.

"Consider me a friend."

"Do you have a name?" McBride presses.

"Call me...'COMMON.'"

"Mr. Common?"

"No, just COMMON is fine."

"So, where is Jones? Is he still alive?"

"Mr. McBride, I think the less you know about this matter, the better it is for you."

"The entire CIA knows he's been grabbed. Do you realize Waxman is in the White House right now, briefing the President?"

"That is of no concern to me. What is your President going to do? Even if he were able to find us, which is doubtful, I don't think he has the stomach to see how extremely dark this situation could get. He's like most Americans, ostriches with their heads in the sand, only looking up when imminent danger is already staring them in the face...and it's too late by then. Otherwise just a lot of talk. You'll see."

"Are you going to kill Jones?" McBride asks.

"Don't worry. You will never see Isaac Jones again. Goodbye."

McBride pulls to the side of the road and stares out the windshield. The phone is still in his hand. He looks down and sees that his hand is shaking. He uses his other hand to steady it. *He better be right,* he thinks. Then another thought comes to him, one that horrifies him to the core: how pissed-off Isaac Jones would be should he escape and find-out it was him who revealed the black location to this mystery man.

He swallows hard and pulls back onto the road, while the drone breaks its formation and returns to base.

Chapter 13

Steven Waxman and Eldon Chase walk down the main hall in the West Wing of the White House, toward the Oval Office, being escorted by a young, focused member of the Secret Service detail. Waxman hangs-up his cell phone.

"General Mooney hasn't found anything yet," he quietly informs Eldon, who nods in understanding.

"And the tracker?"

"Hasn't been activated."

They pass the Roosevelt Room and approach the appointment secretary's desk. Waxman finds it hard *not* to appreciate the history of the White House. *So many decisions that changed the world have happened here*, he thinks to himself.

The secretary is a thin, pleasant looking woman in her 40's, with dark hair pulled up in a bun and reading glasses resting on her nose. "Go right in, gentlemen, they're expecting you."

The accompanying young agent opens the door for the two men and they walk in. This is their first time in the Oval Office with this President. They take it in calmly. The

President is standing, looking out the window at the Rose Garden. Chief of Staff Harrison is seated on a couch next to the President's desk, looking over some papers. They both turn toward the door as the men enter. Harrison arises and greets them with handshakes.

"Steven. Eldon. Thanks for coming." He looks over at the President, who is now walking toward them. "Mr. President, this is Deputy Director Steven Waxman, and you know Eldon Chase."

"Steven," the President says, firmly gripping Waxman's hand.

"Mr. President."

The President releases Waxman's hand and looks at Eldon. "Eldon, how the heck are you, old friend? It's been a long time."

"Ok, considering," Chase answers, with a smile as they shake.

"Please," Harrison says, motioning toward the couch. Waxman and Chase take a seat, while Harrison takes a chair next to the couch and the President sits at his desk. A door opens from the right, not the door Waxman and Chase just entered from, and former CIA Director Ethan Christensen walks in.

"Ah, everyone's here," he says with a smile.

Waxman is surprised to see his former boss and quickly stands to greet him, "Mr. Director, how are you?" He shakes Christensen's hand.

"That's 'former Director', and I'm well, thank you," Christensen turns, and looks at Chase. "Mr. Chase, it's been awhile." They shake hands. "Last time I saw you, I was trying to get you to change your mind about leaving the Agency. I'm glad you're still around." Christensen then looks to the President, and says, referring to Eldon, "This man was one of the best black assets that ever worked for me."

The President smiles.

"Mr. Former Director," Chase says with a smile. "I didn't know you were going to be here, Sir."

"Well, under the circumstances, the President asked me to attend." The men all sit. "Where are we on finding my godson?"

Waxman tells them about his trip to Jones' house and that General Mooney hasn't been able to find any satellite imagery, so far.

"Gentlemen," the President says, "I don't have to tell you how troubling this is. I am on the outside of this situation and it cannot stay that way. Exactly who is Isaac Jones, and why would anyone want to grab him?"

Chase looks over to Waxman, who looks over to Christensen, who looks at Harrison, who looks at the President, as though it were a choreographed revolving scene out of a movie.

The President catches the circle of glances, knowing it means no one wants to start, and says, "Anyone?"

Waxman asks Christensen, "You haven't told him?"

"It was your project, Steven. I didn't want to start without you."

"Project? Steven, tell me!" the President barks, getting a little impatient.

Waxman explains to the President about the Animus Project. He tells him about Senator Thurston and Congressman Lopez, about the Benghazi/Iran mission, about the North Korean mission, and about the Reagan Connection operation. The President sits listening, seemingly without emotion. But Harrison is clearly floored, listening with his mouth falling further ajar with each revelation about Jones.

"Good Lord, this man is a hero! Ethan, Isaac Jones is your godson?!" Christensen nods. Harrison looks at the President who is now standing up, walking around his desk, moving closer to the rest of the men. He gives Waxman a serious look as he towers over him.

"This is quite the dilemma, Steven. You have a black asset engaging in covert actions, in foreign countries, without congressional oversight. You're under the covert direction of a United States Senator and U.S. Congressman, and now your asset has been taken out of a black site by God knows who. How could you let this happen?"

Waxman breaks his gaze away from the President, and looks to the floor, "I'm sorry, Mr. President."

President Mitchell, still looking at Waxman, is stunned. "This has Oversight hearing written all over it. How do I keep my nominee as the next Director of the CIA out of this?"

"Mr. President, I know...what?!" The President's comment sinks-in. "Next Director?" Waxman looks at the President, then over to Christensen who is smiling, then to Harrison who says, "Steven, the President has decided that you are the man he wants to head the CIA, but this Jones issue could be a real problem. We need to do two things. One, we need Jones recovered, alive. Two, no one is to know about this meeting. Now, how do we proceed without using the CIA?"

"I'm not sure I understand. What do you mean 'without using the CIA'?" Waxman asks.

Christensen sits up. "Steven, has it occurred to you that the only one with the information on where Jones was living was Thurston, Lopez, and the CIA database? Do you think Lopez or Thurston sold him out?"

"No," Waxman knowingly shakes his head.

"Then you have a mole in the Agency," Christensen continues. "As far as how we proceed without CIA involvement, do you know who Elliot Warren is?"

"Elliot Warren?" Waxman replies. "He's British Secret Intelligence Service."

"He's due to land in D.C. in less than an hour. He and Jones are friends. As a matter of fact, he was involved in the Iran mission with Jones, and in North Korea, too, right?" Christensen asks.

"Yes, but what is he doing coming here? And how do you know this?" Waxman inquires.

Christensen tilts his head to one side as if to say that was a ridiculous question. "Stella called him," he finally reveals.

Waxman half smiles, not because it was funny that Stella took it upon herself, but that she took action he hadn't thought of. The President interrupts, "Then it's decided. Steven, you and this Elliot Warren will find and rescue Jones. Eldon, I want you with them. Whatever it takes, clean this up tight, and then, Steven, we will move forward with your nomination. Thank you, gentlemen," the President says, dismissing them.

Harrison escorts Waxman and Chase to the door and closes it behind them.

Meanwhile, Christensen quietly advises,
"Mr. President, You know, Lopez and Thurston are going to have to be cut out of this right now. They have to back out. No more involvement in CIA operations."

"I'll handle Lopez and Thurston. Set it up, Gio."

"Yes, Mr. President."

Chapter 14

Isaac Jones sits strapped into a chair in a storage area of a giant cargo ship. He woke-up from his stupor a few minutes ago with a throbbing headache. Disoriented, it takes him a minute to remember what had happened. The last thing he remembers is being moved from the plane to the boat, and now it feels like they're moving. He hears the echoing of footsteps above him as if he is inside a giant shell. Maybe it's his hearing being off, maybe not. A single florescent light attached to the wall above the door lights the room. It's a rusty-walled room with an oily and damp floor. In the distance, he hears the slow drip, drip, drip, of water. He can almost smell the rust. To add insult to injury, the room also smells of urine. Jones considers the strong probability that this ship has been used for human trafficking. He imagines the room filled with scared, hopeless people, cramped together, left to a long journey to an unknown destination overseas. The evidence assaults his senses.

His feet are tied to a metal chair, and his hands are tied behind his back. Jones tries to rock the chair over, but it doesn't budge. He looks down and sees the legs are screwed into the floor. He also notices the back of the chair is resting against another chair behind him, which is empty. It's cold and Jones can see his breath as he exhales. He's still in the jeans and t-shirt he slipped on what now seems like weeks ago. He's still barefoot. His feet are the coldest of all, resting on the damp, metal floor. A shiver pushes itself up his spine.

Jones is startled when the door flies open and thuds against the wall. Two men with hoods over their heads drag another person in by the arms, feet dragging behind. The thin person is dressed in a black, long-sleeved shirt, black BDU-type pants, and black boots. The head is limp and the black hair is in a ponytail. He squints hard to see…it's Yon! They drag her to the empty chair, outside his direct vision, and flop her down.

"Be easy with her!" Jones yells turning his head straining to see her.

The men ignore him, strap Yon to the chair and leave.

Jones can't see Yon since they're back-to-back, but he calls out to her, "Yon, Yon!"

No answer.

FRENCH ALPS, FRANCE

Mr. Hill is seated in a chair in front of Mr. Do-hoyn Park. Park's family is originally from North Korea but escaped to the West shortly after his birth. His father was a member of COMMON before him, and he assumed his father's seat upon his death. He is the unofficial leader of COMMON and its senior member at 82 years of age.

"So, you say Brycekov is working outside the group to manipulate outcomes to benefit his own agenda?" Park asks.

"That's precisely what I am saying," Hill answers.

"And you have proof of this?"

Hill pulls out a pocket recorder and plays the drone-recording of the conversation between McBride and Brycekov:

> *"No, no. Calm down. Just a gut feeling. I could be wrong."*
> *"Who are you?"*
> *"Consider me a friend."*
> *"Do you have a name?"*
> *"Call me...'COMMON.'"*
> *"Mr. Common?"*
> *"No, just COMMON is fine."*

Mr. Park sits up and places his elbows on the desk, with his hands under his chin. "This is quite serious," Park says in an understated tone, "Well, Brycekov knows the consequences of his actions. It's been a long time since we had a situation like this inside the group. We will need to deal with Brycekov. Needless to say, this must stay between us for now, until I decide how to proceed," Park states.

"Fine. If I may, on another issue..."

"Yes?"

"What about Isaac Jones?"

"Jones? What about him?" Park asks with a puzzled tone.

"I was thinking we could help the Americans locate him."

"No, it is of no significance to our interests," Park comments.

"I think it is in our interest, my friend. Jones has been very instrumental in assisting with our interests recently. Surely, he could be of use in the future?"

"Perhaps he could have been, but it doesn't appear that way now. We stay out of it. Jones and the Americans are on their own."

"I understand. Thank you." Hill walks out, feeling frustrated. *That's complete rubbish*, he thinks. *I can't just let him get killed. But if I get involved and Park discovers it...*

He returns to his office and sits at his desk, wondering how the COMMON group moved so far off-track. They now operate more like criminals protecting their own financial assets over the original goal of world stability and promoting western democracies. *I won't just do nothing*. He lets out a sigh, and picks up his encrypted satellite phone.

Hill opens his desk drawer and presses the power button on a signal scrambler. With phone in-hand, he presses a number from his contacts list.

"Hello, Mr. Hill," says the man on the other end.

"Is this line secure?" inquires Mr. Hill.

"Yes, I activated the scrambler on my end as soon as I saw it was you calling. I must say this is highly irregular," former Director Christensen states, matter-of-factly. "I thought we agreed long ago to limit our conversations to encrypted email."

"Yes, I know, old friend, but I have urgent information and don't know who I can trust in the United States government. And I thought it was time we spoke in person."

"I'm listening."

Mr. Hill informs Christensen about Brycekov working outside the interests of the group. Hill explains that during his internal investigation, he discovered Brycekov was the force behind the Reagan Connection mission. He provides Christensen with specific details about how Brycekov contracted with operatives to attack locations of historical significance to former American President Ronald Reagan – operatives from inside the Russian Government. "He didn't need to be paid, he didn't need the money. But he accepted the contract. He is a true believer in communism."

Hill goes on to explain that Brycekov and his men teamed-up with some Islamic extremists to hide Russia's involvement. But when Jones and his team discovered their plan in London, Brycekov's contractors were furious and demanded their money back, $1 million. Brycekov also sought revenge for the loss of his close comrade, Poloski, whom Jones killed during the covert operation in London.

Hill adds that Brycekov had known the North Koreans were still trying to find out what nation state blew up their missile and drone control center in Pyongyang. Brycekov knew Jones and Yon U were responsible, and used back channels to contact North Korea and reveal their names. Kim Jong-Un, himself, ordered the capture, interrogation, and death sentence of Isaac Jones and Yon U. Brycekov gave them the location of Yon, and with McBride's help, the North

Koreans received Jones' location too. "You know what happened next," Mr. Hill ends.

Christensen isn't surprised to hear McBride is the mole. He already suspected him, "Mr. Hill, if what you are telling me is true, this is very disturbing. There are only a handful of people inside the American Government who know about COMMON, and it's in the world's best interest to keep it that way. I had to play dumb when Poloski told Jones he was working for COMMON. We know how you operate and have allowed your organization to operate because of your lengthy history but–"

"Mr. Director, let's stop with the platitudes. You know, as well as I do, that the American Government has no control over my group. Our technology is superior, our intelligence is superior, and our relationships and assets around the world would work against any American aggression against us. So, let's be friends and get to the issue at-hand, shall we?"

Christensen ponders Hill's bold statement in silence. The first key to a good negotiation is control, make your opponent talk more than you do, and you will get twice the information. He sits silently, patiently waiting for Hill to break the impasse.

Hill knows he's talking more than he should…and finally says, "I believe Isaac Jones is a valuable asset and has done extremely good work on behalf of America, and indirectly, my group. It's been a win-win for all of us. Let's just say I feel the need to protect him, I believe it's in our common interest that he be recovered, alive."

Christensen was quietly encouraged and kept his tone calm. "Really? I wonder, is this act of charity coming from the COMMON group as a whole? Or, is there another motive?"

"Now, that is a complicated question. A question I will be glad to answer in the future, but right now it's not a priority topic of discussion."

"Getting my godson back alive is my top priority."

"Your godson? That certainly raises the stakes for needed success now, doesn't it? So this is personal for you. Personal feelings often muddy the well on these types of situations," Hill cautions.

"Perhaps, but the dynamics are set, I can't change them. So, in reality, you are correct. It couldn't get any more personal, Mr. Hill. I don't want any BS. If you are serious about Jones' value and truly want to help, I would be extremely grateful."

"Fair enough. A relationship based on mutual trust, verified by operational success," Hill replies. "So here it is...Jones and the South Korean agent are currently being held on a cargo ship that just left the port of Valdez, Alaska, about an hour ago. They are headed toward Japan. I doubt they will go all the way to North Korea, so I presume they will interrogate them, extract needed Intel, kill them, and then dump their bodies in the Pacific Ocean when they are finished. I suggest you move quickly."

"What is the name of the ship?"

"I do not have that information, but it is black with a red stripe just below the main deck. It should not be too hard to find just off the Alaskan coast. These vessels travel quite slowly," Hill responds.

"Thank you," Christensen says. Setting the phone down and exhaling a large sigh, he wonders if he can trust Hill or if this is all simple misdirection. Regardless, he is out of options, and this appears to be the only direction he has in front of him.

Chapter 15

After a short time, Jones feels Yon squirm and hears her moan as she wakes up.

"Yon?" he whispers. She doesn't answer, but he can tell she is coming out of her drugged state. He whispers again, louder, "Yon!"

In a quiet, sleepy voice, she answers, "Isaac?"

"Yes, I am here. Are you alright?"

"I don't know. Are you alright? How did you get here? How did I get here? Where are we?" Questions are rolling through her awakening mind and off her lips.

"Slow down, Sweetheart, we're alright. How do you feel?"

"I have a terrible headache. What happened?"

"What do you remember?" he asks.

She thinks for a moment, "I was at home and I spotted some men outside my house. They were in full tactical gear, so I braced for an attack. When I saw them moving toward the front of my building, I went out the back. I thought I had lost them. I was hiding in the alley behind my building when I heard one of them talking on his phone. He said your name and I knew we were in trouble. I called you, but that is when they found me. I ran, but they caught me." She pauses, "That's the last thing I remember."

"Could you tell their nationality?"

"I did not recognize any voices, but they were definitely Korean."

"That's what I was afraid of. Someone gave us up to the North Koreans," Jones tells her.

"Who?"

"I don't know, but I'm going to find out. Can you get your hands free?"

Jones feels her trying to get free from her ties, but with no success. "No, they are much too tight," she tells him.

"Can you reach my hands?"

Yon reaches back and finds his hands, "Yes."

"Good. On my left wrist, feel for a small bump."

Yon felt his wrist. "My other left wrist," he says, smirking somewhat. She changes hands and feels the other wrist. The bump is slight but noticeable.

"There?" she asks.

"That's it. Push it and hold for three seconds."

He feels her do as instructed, then she releases the pressure.

"Tracker?" she asks.

"Yeah, I hope the good guys are listening."

LANGLEY, VIRGINIA

Deputy Director Waxman and Eldon Chase are in his office when Stella knocks and enters without waiting for an answer. Elliot Warren trails in right behind her, "Gentlemen, may I please present Elliot Warren of Her Majesty's SIS."

Both men rise from their chairs. Waxman walks over and greets Warren first with a firm handshake. "Elliot, it's great to finally meet you face-to-face."

"Likewise, Sir."

"Please, call me Steven. I found out you were on your way just a short time ago," Waxman says, giving Ms. Stella a knowing look as she leaves the men to talk. She looks back over her shoulder at her boss, who gives her a slight smile as she exits. "This is Eldon Chase. He's an asset location guardian, and former CIA asset."

"Nice to meet you, Mr. Chase," Warren says. "So, you're the one who lost my friend?"

Eldon's face tightens. Warren leans in slowly, almost menacingly, into Eldon's space. Then he leans back and slaps him on the forearm, and says with a laugh, "I'm just hackin' on ya', old boy. We'll get him back! Please, get me up to speed."

Waxman relaxes into his desk and the two guests sit in opposing chairs in front of him. The desk phone buzzes. "Yes, Stella?"

"Ethan Christensen for you. He said it's urgent."

Waxman presses the speaker button on his phone, "Hi, Ethan, you're on speaker with me, Mr. Chase, and Elliot Warren from British SIS."

"Jones and Yon are on a cargo ship that left the port of Valdez, Alaska, about an hour ago, headed east. We're trying to get the name of the vessel, but all we know right now is it's black with a red stripe on the side, no known flag state markings. The ship is slow moving, so you should be able to locate it easily enough."

Waxman stands up. "Who's got them, and how did you get this information?" he asks.

"North Koreans, with help from a Russian agent, and a mole in the CIA."

"Who's the mole?!" Waxman almost yells.

"Not now. We'll deal with that later. For now, don't trust anyone outside of our circle until I figure out how deep this goes. I don't think they're going to take them to North Korea but–"

Waxman interrupts, "They'll interrogate…and then, eliminate."

"Correct, that's the assumption. We've got to get him off that ship before he becomes fish food on the bottom of the Pacific Ocean. How soon can you get moving?"

"How good is this intel?" Warren asks.

"About ninety percent."

"Thanks, Ethan. I'll keep you updated," replies Waxman, closing the line.

Ms. Stella bursts in. "We have a signal from Isaac's tracker!"

"Where?" Waxman asks.

"Somewhere in the North Pacific Ocean. It's tracking toward the East China Sea but moving incredibly slow, too slow to be an airplane, a ship or boat, perhaps."

"That confirms Christensen's tip," Waxman states.

Chase and Warren nod toward each other. "Well, Mr. Chase," Warren says, "shall we dance?"

Chase smiles with a nod, "You lead and I'll follow."

NORTH PACIFIC OCEAN

Two men burst into the holding area and rush directly toward Jones. One man pulls out a taunt military switchblade from his front pocket and flips it open with a snap. He cuts Jones' ties and they lift him roughly from his chair and start searching him. Jones notices that neither man holds a gun, *First mistake*, he smiles. *Game on!*

The man with the knife demands, "Where is it?" speaking in English for the first time.

"Where's what?" Jones asks.

"The tracker you activated!"

Taking advantage of being unbound Jones quickly drops low and swings his left leg around in a scissor stance, knocking the man with the knife off his feet, sending his body crashing to the floor. Jones levels up and kicks the man other man in the stomach with all of his might, causing the man to curl up in pain. The switchblade owner lunges at Jones. Jones deflects the blade by swiping the man's arm and delivers a crushing blow to the man's face. The man stumbles back and Jones kicks a severe blow to his stomach, causing him to hit the floor. Jones rushes him, easily deflecting a weak knife swipe by kicking the man's hand. The knife flies out of his hand and lands a few feet away. Jones grabs the man in a choke-hold, then with all his might he pulls him up by the neck, and over his side, causing the man to fly over the top of him. Jones uses their full body weights to drop them to the ground. Jones feels the man's neck pop, and body goes limp.

Jones releases the grip and hears Yon yell, "Isaac!" She is straining her neck, turning to see what is going on.

He looks and sees the remaining man coming toward him. Jones scans the floor, finding the knife just a few feet from him. He rolls to it, grasps the handle, and turns over swiftly, throwing the knife which finds its target, lodging deep into the man's throat. The man makes a garbling noise, then blood spits from his mouth. His eyes look confused, and then distant, as he falls to the floor.

Jones walks over to the body, bends over the dead man and slowly removes the knife from the man's neck. He wipes the blood from blade on the man's pant leg and turns toward Yon. She smiles up at him. "It's about time you went all Rambo and got us out of here."

Jones smiles. "I was waiting for you, but since you were being a slacker, I figured I better get the job done."

He cuts her binds, she stands up, and they embrace. Jones pulls back from the hug and looks into her eyes. "Are you alright?"

"I am."

"Let's get out of here."

Chapter 16

At least we know he's still alive, Stella thinks. She squints at her computer screen, staring intently as the blinking green dot in the middle of a map shows his current location. It's a strong signal, but it hasn't moved in ten minutes. She wonders if they've stopped in the middle of the ocean. *They must be on a ship*, she thinks.

The phone on her desk rings and she answers, "Deputy Director Waxman's office."

"Hi, Aunt Stella!" A young voice with a slight Middle Eastern accent responds.

Stella is taken off-guard momentarily. "Michael, how are you?" she asks of Jones' son.

"I'm good. I've been trying to get ahold of my dad, but he's not answering his phone. He usually sends me an email if he's going to be working out of town, but I haven't heard from him. Do you know where he is?"

Stella lets out a deep breath. "Oh, Michael, I don't know where he is exactly, but I'm sure everything is fine. I am sure he will call you when he can. Don't you worry," she says, not wanting to lie.

"You don't know where he is?"

"Oh, I know where he is. I'm looking at his location right now," she says, staring at the green dot on her computer screen.

"Ok, so he's working. I wonder why he didn't tell me he was going to be out working."

"It was a last-minute thing. You know how his job is."

Michael sounds disappointed. "Yeah. Well, ok, if you talk to him, will you tell him I called and just wanted to say 'Hi'?"

"Absolutely! How's school going?" she tries to change the subject.

"Fine, it's strict here, and the math is horrible, but the pizza's great. Also, the Headmaster's pretty strict. I think my dad ought to talk with him. Umm, here he comes, I better go."

"Michael?"

"Yes?

"Your dad will be home soon, alright?"

"Ok, bye!"

Stella gets up and walks into Waxman's office just as he is hanging up his phone. Chase and Warren are still seated in front of his desk. She tells the three men, "The tracker is still transmitting, so whoever has him either doesn't have the technology to pick up the signal or they must not have noticed."

"I find that hard to believe," Chase comments.

"My sentiments, exactly," adds Warren. "Shy of these people not knowing who they have in Jonesy, my educated guess is that something else has happened…and Jonesy, himself, may be the reason for the change. His nature is to interfere."

"And by 'interfere' you mean that he's possibly free, on board?" Eldon asks.

"Indeed, it's possible."

Waxman relays the phone conversation he just completed, "General Mooney was able to locate a satellite covering Idaho last night. He located the van travelling at a high rate of speed from Jones' safe house traveling to a small industrial airport in a much smaller town of Caldwell, Idaho. The van was abandoned there. He had the local FBI check it out." Everyone looks up at Waxman, surprised. "Don't worry, I know this FBI guy. He owes me a favor and I called him and he promised to keep it quiet. Anyway, the van was clean. Mooney then traced to flight to Alaska where they found another van abandoned at the port. I haven't done anything with it yet besides ask the Alaska State Police to secure the premises and hold the van."

"Stella, get a bird fueled up and ready to go to our base in Alaska. From there we'll need a helicopter and a Navy runner on standby. Once you guys are there you can decide to go by air or boat. Any thoughts?" Waxman asks.

"Stella, how long is the flight?" Warren inquires.

"With the fuel stop in Seattle, a little over ten hours."

"That's too bloody long. Those blokes aren't going to hold him for ten hours before dumping him," Warren states emphatically.

"We can't change our geography. Let's just get moving!" Waxman says.

"No, we can't change OUR geography but, we can enlist some help closer than we are."

"What do you mean?"

"Oliver Riley."

Warren knew Riley was training American Military in Alaska, but didn't want to suggest to Waxman that they bring him in until the right moment.

"What about Oliver Riley?" Waxman asks, looking at Stella, who returns a slight shrug of her shoulders.

"Who's Oliver Riley?" Chase asks.

"He's a down-under chap who's worked missions with Jonesy and me for years. Former Australian Secret Intelligence Service, and now a private contractor."

Chase smiles a slight smile and looks at Warren, "Great, another Brit brother..."

Warren responds, "He's Australian...more like a second cousin who's just been paroled from prison." This makes both men chuckle.

"He was on the Iran/Benghazi mission, remember?" Both Waxman and Stella nod. "He might be able to get eyes on. If things appear to get out of control before we arrive, he can intervene."

"The boat's already left the Alaskan harbor," Stella states.

"Maybe first he can go through the abandoned van Mooney said they left, checking to see if they missed something that might give us an idea where they're headed. Second, we may be able to use him on the seas."

"But, if he gets spotted, things could go wrong fast," Stella adds with concern.

"Things are already a wretched mess. We need his help on this," Warren says.

"Pull him in, but keep it quiet. If he needs to intervene before you guys arrive, it needs to be stealth. This has to be off-the-books, understand?" Waxman directs.

"No problem. I got this, Guv'nor," Warren says in the worst Aussie accent he can pretend to muster, and then smiles at Stella, attempting to give her reassurance, it doesn't work. She frowns and walks out of the Director's office. She plops down in her chair, shaking her head. *I hope these gun-toting cowboys don't muddle it up.*

123

Chapter 17

President Mitchell sits at his desk in the Oval Office. He's seldom alone in this room. Being President of the most powerful country in the world is harder, but more satisfying, than he had ever imagined. It's a job he doesn't take lightly, or for granted. In the last election, the American people entrusted him to lead and protect them. He knows he's the right person for the job, and believes God has put him in the right place, at the right time, in history. The economy quickly improved after he lowered taxes on individuals and on corporations, which seemed to once again prove that Reagan was right. Job growth was rising, and family incomes right along with it. Government doesn't seem as broken as it did just a few years ago, and even Congress' approval ratings have gone up.

There remain many more issues on his plate, though.

The main issue that disturbs him the most is terrorism. It's both a national security issue and a political hot-button, and despite all the good that's coming from his policies, terrorism is the one issue that could make or break him winning a second term. He doesn't look at it as just a political issue. He takes it personally. The American people elected him to keep the homeland safe, which is always their first priority – and he knows it.

Mitchell often wonders how George W. Bush, and later Barack Obama, decided when to take action, when to support or to stay out of foreign affairs. The two men stood in such contrast to each other. They couldn't have been further away on the spectrum.

He wonders if the right answer lies somewhere in the middle. Bush went after the 9/11 hijackers without hesitation. Obama seemingly refused to confront ISIS, or even call them Islamic Extremists. How could Americans have elected two men, so polar opposite of each other, in such a short period of time? Are the American people really so fickle? Or was the Iraq war so draining that Americans found themselves longing for a change of attitude to see if that made things better? Mitchell wonders if he, himself, now is that middle ground. He knows he could pick up the phone and call either one of those past Presidents for advice, but so far has decided against it. He trusts his advisors and his instinct. His wife told him once, "Complicated issues don't have easy solutions – though they may have simple ones. I know you will make the right decisions if you listen to your heart and trust your mind."

Mitchell starts each day with a daily briefing on threats, and has not missed one briefing since being sworn in. It's the foreign terrorism issue that keeps him feeling slightly unsure at times. He is a staunch supporter of Israel, to him that's a no-brainer. He would always stand by Israel and all of America's allies without hesitation. However, covert actions have been something he has stayed away from so far, even against some of his top advisor's recommendations. Covert ops, if done successfully, have a great impact on the security of the nation, without the nation even knowing about it. Although, if the operation goes bad, Congress and the news media share the same response: *scandal.* It's ugly business, and more and more it seems necessary. He has known for some time that he will eventually have to authorize some covert action, on a limited scale, to protect America's interests. It seems that this Isaac Jones might be the right man, if Waxman and his team can get him back.

This brings another thought to mind. What do we do when Jones is rescued? There must be a response to whoever kidnapped a CIA asset in a CIA black location. *We can't just let it go*, he thinks. He decides to take it one step at a time; get Jones back, and see what Waxman suggests for a response.

One thing Mitchell is sure of, the *Animus Project*, as it is now being run, will end. Senator Thurston and Congressman Lopez are out. He had his Chief of Staff set up a meeting with them for later today. He's expecting push-back from Thurston, but he and Lopez know each other pretty well and he doubts any argument will come from the Congressman. Either way, they're out, and he will decide if Isaac Jones will continue to work covertly. If he does allow Jones to continue, it will be at under his direct authority, period!

The quietness of the Oval Office allowed the President to clearly recall the discussion he had with his Chief of Staff about the possibility of Jones continuing to perform covert ops. Harrison warned that if the President approves any such action, he loses plausible deniability. Mitchell's response was simply, "So be it. That's the way I want it. These actions have to be supervised."

"That's what oversight committees are for," Harrison challenged.

"You know as well as I do that these operations fall outside of congressional preview. Oversight committees don't even know about the operations. There is no oversight, unless something goes wrong and someone's head is on the chopping block," the President responded.

"Better someone else's head than yours."

"Don't go there, Gio. IF Jones is brought back alive and IF we decide to continue his covert status, I have to be in the loop. I need you to support me on this."

"Yes, Mr. President."

ANCHORAGE, ALASKA

Oliver Riley fits his Australian background. At 6'1" and 200 pounds, his muscular frame has a deft rhythm about it. He's got a glint in his eyes and a constant smirk across his face. His dark hair is shoulder length and parted down the middle falling lazily to each side. Since leaving the Australian Secret Intelligence Service and going into private contracting, he's let his once-regulation haircut go. It's almost Mullet-long but not quite, though no one in his right mind would make a snide remark about it. He likes it long and doesn't care what other people think. He's done tours in Iraq and Afghanistan and the premature aging in his face shows the toll it's taken on him. "Ah, but at least I'm not bald, like so many of you mates," he often tells his comrades.

Riley travels around the globe training military and private security officers, and makes more than a good living at it. Every once in a while, he takes a private contract and does the dirty work governments won't officially involve themselves in. He has strict rules though: only work for pro-democracy governments, no assassinating world leaders or celebrities, never take a revenge contract, and no failing. If he takes a job, it's only when he's confident he can guarantee success.

Today, Riley is at Fort Richardson Army Base in Alaska, working with a special unit of Army Rangers. He's fond of Army Rangers. They are tough, no-nonsense, get-'er-done kinds of guys and they take their job seriously. He met Isaac Jones in Desert Storm when Jones was serving as a Ranger. They've been close friends ever since.

No sooner had Warren's call come in to Riley about Jones, than Riley did something he never does; he told the Commander that he needed to cancel the rest of the training to deal with an emergency. The Commander was furious, and for a moment Riley thought it might make things better if he revealed that he was going to assist on a mission sanctioned by President Mitchell. He decided otherwise and kept his mouth shut. He knows he can reconnect later with the Commander and smooth things over.

Warren briefly explained that he is in the U.S., at the CIA headquarters in Langley, meeting with Deputy Director Waxman. Purely because Jones is in imminent danger, the President authorized him to help, and gave clearance to bring in Riley. Riley said he would return the call as he left the base.

Just outside the gates, he picks up his phone and dials.

"It's about bloody time!" Warren answers.

"What's happened?"

Warren unpacks the details about Jones being grabbed out of the safe house, and Yon being taken around the same time from her home. He goes on to give Riley details about Jones' kidnappers flying him to Seattle, then to Alaska.

"Yon U? That Bird we saw him with in North Korea?" Riley asks.

"Affirmative."

When Jones and Yon were working together on the North Korean mission, Warren and Riley showed-up in the middle of the fight. Jones had to convince them to leave before one of them got caught or killed. He feared it might cause an international crisis if American, South Korean, Australian, and British agents were found working covertly in North Korea, even though all of them were sent separately by their own governments.

"Jones and Yon are on a cargo ship that left the port of Valdez, Alaska, about two hours ago, headed into the Pacific Ocean toward the East China Sea. It's slow moving, so it shouldn't be too far out of port. American FBI has the van Jones was transported in. They're holding it for you to check," Warren informs him.

"Slowdown, who took them?"

"We think the North Koreans, with help from a Russian agent...and a CIA mole."

"What?! Is there a lead on the mole?"

"Not yet. The good news is that Jones activated his tracker, and we have a strong signal, so we can lead you right to him. I'm on my way now," Warren says.

"You're on a plane?" Riley asks.

"Yes, the CIA was kind enough to supply me with a cute, little Gulfstream IV, along with my old pal, Henry. This chap makes the best cup of coffee ever, it reminds me of Sir Colin William's, a coffee shop in Manchester. Took out a Russian network asset in the bathroom there once..." Warren says to Riley as he holds up his cup toward Henry, asking for a refill. Henry nods in understanding.

"Nice. You Brits get all the special treatment."

"Hey, complements of Uncle Sam!"

"So, it's just you? No offense but..."

"I've got an old-timer named Chase who's with me. But other than that, we're on our own. The President wants this low key," Warren explains.

"Do we know how many are holding him?"

"No."

"You're still going to be a while. I might have to grab a couple of 'mechanics' to help me until you arrive," Riley informs Warren.

"It's your call, just make sure they silently 'tune the engine.'"

"I'll tell you, Mate, it's not going to be a cracker of a day. Even in that jet, you're hours away. I might have to move without you. It doesn't sound like they're gonna catch-and-release. Jones' time is limited. He could already be dead," Riley says soberly.

"I understand, but as long as that tracker is transmitting, I'm operating as if he's alive. Do what you need to, and keep me updated."

"Copy that. See you soon." Riley hangs-up his phone, and flips a U-turn heading back toward the base.

It's a five-hour drive from Anchorage to Valdez, but by air he could be there in just over 30 minutes. *I need two good Rangers and a chopper*, he thinks as he builds his strategy.

Chapter 18

T rent McBride is sitting at his desk reviewing reports trying to keep busy. He pushes the button for Hillary, "Get me Chief of Staff Harrison on the line, please."

McBride hasn't received any updates since he returned from his drive. He's still irritated that Harrison wouldn't let him come to the briefing with Waxman and the President. Now he's out of the loop. He thought he would casually ask Harrison how the meeting went and perhaps find out what action, *if any*, the President has authorized.

His phone buzzes, "He's unavailable," Hillary tells him.

"What do you mean 'unavailable'?"

"I don't know. His secretary just said he was unavailable."

"Alright," he says. "Try former Director Christensen."

"Christensen? Really?" She knows Christensen loathes McBride.

"Just try him, Hillary. Now."

A minute later she buzzes McBride back, "All I got was voicemail. I didn't leave a message. Do you want me to call back and ask him to call you when he can?"

"No," he says, standing up, resolving he may have to talk with Waxman. Waxman is emotionally attached to Jones, and McBride really wants to talk to a neutral party, but his lust for information is too great. He walks out of his office. "I'll be at Waxman's office for a few minutes. If Harrison calls back, put him on-hold and buzz Stella to let me know," he instructs Hillary as he walks by, without waiting for an answer.

As he walks down the sterile halls of the CIA, he thinks, *I have to get my arms around this situation. Somehow I have to make the President see my leadership qualities. I will be the next Director of this Agency. Once Jones is confirmed dead, I'll offer to organize a team to locate and bring to justice those responsible.* He smiles at this thought. *Perhaps this little incident will not only rid me of Jones, but it might be just the thing to propel me forward.*

He rounds the corner, "Hello, Stella," he says smugly.

Stella looks up from her monitor in surprise. "Um, hello, Mr. McBride. I'll announce you," she says standing-up.

"Don't bother. I'll let myself in." Without missing a step, McBride walks right to Deputy Director Waxman's door and opens it, hoping to catch Waxman working on whatever the Jones recovery mission is.

Waxman, seated at his desk, looks up from a file. McBride walks in and plops himself down in the chair right in front of him. Stella follows behind with an apologetic face. Waxman waves to her that it's o.k. and to leave them alone. She closes the door behind her as she exits.

"So, where are we on this Jones issue? How did the meeting at the White House go?" McBride asks.

Waxman sets the file down. "Come in, and make yourself comfortable, Trent."

"Thank you, I just did." McBride puts both elbows on the arms of the chair with his hands clasped against his body, like he is ready to be briefed. He waits for Waxman to start. Silence. The men just sit there, looking at each other. After Waxman makes no reply, McBride smiles, "Well?"

Waxman straightens up in his seat, "I'm sorry, that meeting was 'Room only', and I'm not authorized to discuss it with anyone except those who were in attendance. Frankly Sir, it's classified."

McBride's hands drop, and he leans forward. "'Classified'? I have Top Secret clearance. I am your immediate supervisor, and I want to know what was said in that meeting."

Waxman sits back in his chair, clearly not intimated by his boss's statement. "WE work for the President of the United States. The President gave me strict orders not to discuss the contents of our meeting with anyone, and I'm going to follow those orders."

McBride lets out a sigh of anger and frustration, and he leans in closer, "You know, Steven, I've tolerated your insubordination for quite a long time now, but frankly, I'm getting tired of it. Give me one reason why I shouldn't just fire your ass right now and have you escorted out of the building," McBride fires-back.

A large smile forms on Waxman's face. "Trent, you can't fire me, and you know it."

"Oh, yes, I can."

Waxman steps out from behind his desk, like he is ready for a fight, and glares at McBride. "You could try, and the President would be all over you like white on rice. I'm in the middle of a presidential-ordered mission. The White House is overseeing this entire operation from the Oval Office, and I'm the point man. So, go ahead, fire me and see what happens. And if you want to know what the President said in our 'Classified' meeting, go ask him yourself. Otherwise, get the hell out of my office…Sir."

McBride stays seated, defying Waxman for a moment, shaking his head from side to side. He knows he can't fire Waxman, despite how much he wants to. That would be political suicide. He bluffed to get the information he needed, but Waxman called him on it. He decides he'll deal with Waxman after he's named Director. He slowly rises, "Perhaps you're right. I should have just asked the President myself." He turns and walks toward the door, but stops short, looks back, and says, "Good luck on the mission."

"Drop-in anytime."

McBride leaves the room, closing the door firmly. He walks passed Stella without saying a word, and returns to his office. As he passes Hillary, he asks, "Did Harrison call back?"

"No, Sir."

"Call him again. Tell him it's important." He closes the door behind him, and sits at his desk...seething with anger.

After a few moments Hillary buzzes his phone, "Still unavailable."

McBride slowly drops his forehead on his desk.

NORTH PACIFIC OCEAN

Jones and Yon stand at the door, listening for sounds on the other side. Armed with only the dead guard's knife, Jones knows they are miserably outgunned. It's dark by the door. Jones looks through the shadows at Yon, "You ready?"

She looks up into his eyes, "I'm so sorry. I should have called you sooner, maybe—"

Jones breaks in, taking her hands into his, "It's not your fault. I know you called as soon as you could."

"I'm glad you're here. I don't know what I would do if I were here alone."

Jones smiles, lowers his face to hers, and they kiss. She says through a smile, "You know what this reminds me of?"

"North Korea?"

She laughs, "Yes. Hopefully, I won't get shot this time!"

Jones puts his hand on the door handle.

"How's Michael?" she asks.

He pulls his hand back from the handle, and looks at her, surprised and confused that she's starting a conversation when they are about to step into danger. With a crooked smile he tells her, "He's fine. Grades are good. You know, he's smart as a whip. When we get done here you should come and see him."

"I think I might just do that, Mr. Jones." She lifts her hand to his face, and strokes his cheek softly with one finger.

"Are you purposely trying to distract me, Ms. U?" He takes her hand from his face and gently kisses her palm.

"I've missed you," she says.

"When this is all over, I want you to come back to the States with me. We need to–" His words are interrupted by the sound of someone outside the door. The conversation stops.

Jones motions for her to move to the other side while he crouches down, with the knife up and ready to strike whoever comes through. As the door swings open, a lone figure walks in, missing Jones crouched down in the dark, and Yon now behind the open door. He walks in, expecting to see his comrades still searching Jones for the tracker. Not seeing anyone, he curiously steps forward.

As the guard passes through the doorway, Yon slams it shut quickly. The man, who is about the same size as Jones, jumps with surprise, turning in Yon's direction. He has a rifle hanging down from his shoulder on a strap. Jones seizes the opportunity and grabs the man's head, one hand on each side, and twists with all his might, cracking his neck. Drool falls from the man's mouth as quickly as he falls to the ground.

"We gotta move," Jones says, picking up the rifle, handing it to Yon.

Chapter 19

LANGLEY, VIRGINIA

The phone on Trent McBride's desk buzzes. Hillary's voice comes on, "Sir, Chief of Staff Harrison is returning your call."

McBride sits up quickly and picks up the receiver. "Mr. Harrison, how are you, Sir?"

"It's a busy day, Trent. What can I do for you?" Harrison responds, sounding as irritated as he feels.

"I understand. I was just wondering how the Jones meeting went."

"It went fine, thanks. That it?" Harrison curtly replies.

"Um, well, yes. I just wanted to make sure Steven was giving you all that you need. But I must tell you, as his superior, I'm a little uncomfortable not knowing what's going on. You know since the Director retired, I'm in charge over here. If something goes wrong, it falls in my lap, Sir," he answers, trying to fish for more information.

"I see," Harrison says with a slight chuckle. "You must have asked Steven about the meeting and he wouldn't tell you anything, right?"

A big smile comes across Harrison's face. *I like Waxman more every day*, he thinks to himself.

Wanting to make it sound like he supports Waxman, McBride says, "Well, you know Steven, he's very black and white. So when the President said the briefing was strictly for those in the room, he took it literally. I understand his thinking, but I'm sure the President didn't mean I shouldn't know, considering, technically, I'm his boss."

"Well, you're wrong; it was for the 'room only,'" Harrison states with force. "The President said exactly what he meant. No one is to be in on the details of the Jones operation, including you," Harrison pauses. "The President expects you to stay out of Waxman's way and leave him alone. Right now, he's not working for you, he's working directly on orders from the White House. Let me be more specific: if you hinder Steven Waxman's ability to do his job you will have to answer directly to the President of the United States. Do you understand?"

McBride is pressed back into his seat, and replies with a sheepish "Yes, Sir."

"Anything else? I'm quite busy today."

"No. Thank you."

"*Alrighty then.* I'm glad we understand each other. Hey, why don't you take a few days off? Go home and relax. It'll do you some good."

The phone goes dead. McBride sits up and places it back in its carriage. "Yes, Sir," he says out loud to no one.

At the other end of the CIA headquarters, a quite different conversation is unfolding. "The President is going to nominate you as CIA Director? I'm gob smacked...that's amazing! How do you feel about it? " Stella asks Waxman, sitting in a chair in front of his desk.

"That's what he said. I'm...what did you say... *Gob smacked,* too. I simply am stunned...and, POTUS also said after we get Isaac back, HE would let us know the future of the Animus program, so it looks like I'll soon be faced with that dilemma, too."

"What?" Stella replies, even more shocked. "What do you think he will decide? Continue it, or belly-up? And what will Isaac say?"

"I think the President understands the value of black operations. As far as how Jones will react, I think we need to get him back to find out."

"Yes, agreed. Oh, Michael called me. He was looking for his father."

"What did you tell him?" Waxman asks with a concerned look on his face.

"Just that I was sure his dad was fine and I would have him call as soon as I saw him." A sense of sadness suddenly comes over Stella's face.

"Ok. Keep an eye on that tracker. We'll get him back, Stella. Warren is in route, and he called in that Aussie, Riley, to help. You know both these guys get results, it's how they're wired, and why Jones works with them."

"Yes, but if anything happens to Isaac..." she pauses. "Michael is just a boy, he would be devastated."

"It'll be fine. These guys are pros. Isaac trusts them, and they know he would do the same if the roles were reversed."

THE WHITE HOUSE

Senator James Thurston sits on one of the couches in the Oval Office, nervously tapping his right index finger on the arm of the couch. Every President has the room redecorated after they take office, but for the most part, the setup is the same. The President's desk sits in front of the three thin windowpanes that stretch all the way to the ceiling, each of which is hugged slightly by plush curtains. This President kept his predecessor's color scheme of gold with matching gold tassels hanging down the right side. President Mitchell ordered a slightly smaller oak desk to replace the oversized desk of his predecessor. He felt it looked pompous, so he had it donated to the former President's library.

Just in front of the desk, woven into the carpet, is the official seal of the President of the United States. Beyond that sit two plush, comfortable, tan couches, each facing the other, with a cherry wood coffee table between them. On the far end of each couch are cherry wood end tables, each supporting matching lamps with gold lamp shades. Just off to the side of each couch, at the far side of the office, furthest from the President's desk, are two oversized leather chairs that face the couches. Everyone knows the chair to the left is the one the President sits in during meetings.

Thurston is seated on the couch to the right of the President's desk, deep in thought. He doesn't know why he's been called to this meeting with the President, and he has never been one to enjoy surprises. He's been in the Oval Office numerous times over the years, but today is the first time he's been in the office with this particular President. He looks around, appreciating the rich history of the room. *People think that the greatest men who ever lived have occupied this room*, he thinks to himself. Then snorts out loud, "Well, some greater than others, and some, just darned lucky." He's shaken from his thoughts when the door opens. He stands up, expecting to see the President, but is shocked when Congressman Raul Lopez is escorted in by the President's social secretary. She closes the door behind her, leaving the two men alone in the Oval Office. Lopez looks just as surprised.

Thurston looks over to make sure the door is closed, but knows full-well the room is video recorded 24/7. He then walks over to Lopez, extending his hand, and whispers with a raised eyebrow, "What the hell is going on?"

"I have no idea," Lopez says, forcing a smile for the camera.

"Something tells me this is about Isaac Jones."

"If it is, we're both screwed! You know that, right? I warned you..." Lopez squeezes out between clenched teeth.

"Just relax. What did they say when you were invited to this meeting?" Thurston asks, as they both bend at the waist, looking down at the carpet, moving to seat themselves on the left tan couch.

"Just that the POTUS requested to see me right away, that it was extremely important. I asked what it's about, and the secretary told me she didn't know."

"Same here."

The door opens again and President Mitchell and Chief of Staff Harrison walk in. Both legislators rise. The President smiles, extending his hand to the men, "Ah, Raul...James. Thank you both for coming." The men shake hands with the President. "You both know my Chief of Staff, Giovanni Harrison, right?" he asks motioning toward Harrison.

"Only by reputation," Thurston says, shaking hands with Harrison.

"We've met. Good to see you, again," Lopez says, shaking Harrison's hand.

"Sit, sit," the President says, motioning the men to the couch on the right as he and Harrison sit facing them in the leather chairs. The door opens and a young woman, wearing a brown pant suit, with her long brown hair pulled back, walks in carrying a silver tray with four gold cups and a large pot. She sets the tray down on the coffee table. "Thanks, Loretta." She smiles as if to say "you're welcome" while she pours a cup for the President and hands it to him. She looks at Harrison, who declines a cup, then exits without a word.

"I ordered coffee. Have some?" Both men decline. The President takes a sip and sets the cup down. "I bet you're both wondering why I've asked you here today."

Chapter 20

Oliver Riley is on a three-way video-conference from Alaska, with Waxman, at the CIA headquarters, and Warren, who is still in-flight. Each man's face takes-up a third of the screen. Ms. Stella sits in the chair in front of Waxman's desk, with interest in the conversation.

Riley fills them in. "Ok, those FBI guys weren't much help. They were holding the van when we arrived, but said they didn't find anything, no fingerprints, nothing. They seemed irritated that they had to stay with the van until we arrived. I checked the back of the van and look what I found," he said, holding up a gold chain.

Waxman motions for Stella to come over and look at the monitor. She pauses, taking-in the image on the screen. "That's Isaac's!" she says, pointing to the monitor. "He never takes it off."

Eldon Chase moves next to Warren, into view of the video camera. "She's right. I've seen him many times with that on."

"You said, 'we arrived.' Who's with you, Oliver?" Warren asks.

"A couple of Army Ranger pals of mine from the fort here. They can be trusted, and I need their help. And if these mossies are North Koreans, I'll need to move before you get here."

"Alright. Stella, is the tracker still active?" Warren asks.

"Yes, it's barely moved. They must be in a very slow-moving ship."

"Copy that. Oliver?"

"Ok, we've got a chopper on loan from the base and thought we would go take a looksee," he answers.

"Don't get too close. I don't want you to spook 'em. Do you have high powered vision?" Waxman asks.

"Got it covered, mate. We'll be in the air within the hour," Riley responds.

NORTH PACIFIC OCEAN

Jones cracks the door scanning for threats. Seeing none, he opens it. He and Yon step into the narrow hall. Jones has the knife in his right hand and Yon holds the newly-acquired automatic rifle in front of her, both ready for any threat that might emerge. They are trained killers, and it's comforting to both of them that they've worked together before. They know how each other operates, so eye contact and hand signals are enough as they move down the hallway.

The hallway is dark, with clamshell-covered lights intermittently placed along the wall, just about six-feet from the deck. The bulbs couldn't be more than 40 watts, so the low light and narrow hall feel like standing in a metal tomb. With a little a brighter light toward the end of the hallway, Jones sees a set of stairs leading up from there. He motions Yon to move in that direction.

Together, they slowly work their way up the hall toward the light, hugging the sides of the walls, one on each side, scanning ahead and behind for threats. As they reach the metal staircase, each takes a side and looks up. The stairwell is empty, but they hear footsteps above them. They crouch down into the shadows. The footsteps continue away from them.

Using signals, Jones tells Yon he's going up and she is to follow; she nods. Jones puts his foot on the first step and starts up, Yon is right behind him. As she looks up, she can't resist the temptation, and reaches up and gives Jones a light pat on the fanny. Jones stops in mid-step, he leans back, giving her a half-serious look that says "knock-it-off," and makes a slicing motion with his hand. She smiles playfully, while slightly shrugging her shoulders. Jones shakes his head with a bemused smile, turns, and starts moving up the stairs again.

Jones peeks over the top of the stairs, with just the tip of his head and eyes showing. This area of the ship is much brighter than the lower level they are leaving, and Jones' eyes need a few seconds to adjust. This is the upper level, and Jones can see the sunshine blazing in from the windows. The sun is warm, but the gulf wind is crisp, cool, with the smell of the ocean. No one is in sight. There are large crates and boxes in the room, but nothing gives him any more information as to exactly where they are. There are two open doors, one to the right, one to the left.

Jones steps up all the way into the room, with Yon following right behind.

"So, what's the plan, hot shot?" Yon asks.

"Let's find an emergency raft and throw it over without anyone seeing us, and just float away."

"Do you really think it's going to be that easy?" she asks, raising an eyebrow.

"No. No, I don't. But…let's see what happens," he says, walking toward the door on the left. As they enter the doorway, rifle fire plasters the walls around them. Jones ducks and retreats, rolling behind the wall for cover. Having only the knife, he looks for Yon, knowing she has a firearm. His eyes burst wide open, and his heart sinks as he sees Yon lying on the ground.

"Yon!" Jones yells. He notices blood seeping from her right arm. Shots are still flying above them.

"Damn it," she says in a low voice.

"Do you have the rifle?"

"I dropped it."

The gunfire stops. Jones turns from Yon and looks at the doorway, directly in front of them. A half-a-dozen men enter with their automatic rifles trained on them. From behind them, another half-a-dozen men appear. Jones drops the knife and holds both hands up, showing he's unarmed.

Two men grab him by the arms and lift him to his feet. Another man pulls Jones' hands behind his back and ties them with plastic zip-tie cuffs. Two other men lift Yon up forcefully. She lets out a cry of pain.

"Don't touch her, she's wounded!" Jones yells, letting his free right foot land a hard blow on the Korean guard's face, knocking him to the ground. Another man strikes Jones in the stomach with the butt of his rifle, knocking the wind out of him.

"Enough, Mr. Jones! Why all the dramatics?" a voice asks.

A man appears from the shadows. The reaction of the men clearly indicate he is in-charge, and open a path for him to walk.

"She needs medical attention," Jones says. He doesn't recognize the man, but he is tall and husky. He's Asian and is wearing a North Korean military uniform.

"Medical attention won't change her fate...or yours, for that matter," the man coldly informs Jones.

The boss quickly removes his handgun from its holster and slams it hard against the back of Yon's head; she falls to the floor.

"You bastard!" Jones shakes violently, unsuccessfully attempting to break free from the men holding him tight.

The boss instructs his men, "Throw her overboard!" The men drag her out of the room, leaving a trail of blood.

Jones turns to the man holding his left arm and head-butts him, causing him to release the arm. Jones shakes free of the other man and lowers his shoulder, charging at the man whose head he just slammed. He hits him hard like a linebacker, causing them both to fall to the ground. As he starts to get up, a shot rings-out, ricocheting from the floor just inches from his head. He stops and looks up at the boss, "You didn't have to kill her you son-of-a–"

"Mr. Jones," the Korean interrupts, "I have been waiting a long time for this...too long."

"What are you talking about? I don't even know you," Jones retorts.

"You are right, we have never met. When my government confirmed it was the Americans who blew up our facility, and specifically, you and that woman. They authorized me to send a message back. Actually, I volunteered because you knew my brother. You killed him, and today we will send a message back to your government to not mess in our affairs. And I'll get the satisfaction of killing the man who killed my brother."

Jones looked at the man with confusion. "Your brother? Who was your brother?"

"You might remember him, tall like me, and wore an eye patch over his left eye."

Jones pauses, "Soju? So, this is about revenge?"

"To my government, it's non-diplomatic 'communication' between us and America. But for me, personally…yes, I suppose 'revenge' works, too."

Jones locks eyes with the man, "If you let her die, and I'll send you to the hell your brother now inhabits."

The Korean smacks Jones hard, this time with his own swift, well-planted, but much harder, head-butt. Jones crumbles to the floor.

"Take him back to the cell," the boss orders.

Chapter 21

"Isaac Jones," President Mitchell said, as he set down his cup of coffee. "You both know him, right?" The President picks up a pad and pencil, then lays them casually on his lap.

Thurston and Lopez look at each other, not answering. More importantly, they shift their gazes away from the President.

The President clearly notices the hesitation and awkwardness from the men. "Well, let's cut to the chase, shall we? I know you both know him, and I know about Animus, or the project code-named Animus, and I now also know about Isaac Jones."

"Mr. President, there are some things that are better if you don't know about," Thurston begins. The President's eyes cut him off, mid-sentence. His face isn't angry, just deadly serious.

Thurston collects himself and tries to continue. "For your own good. It's called 'plausible deniability.' Sir, Isaac Jones started working these missions before you became President." Once again, President Mitchell's eyes shut down the attempted conversation.

Lopez doesn't say a word, deciding to let the Senator cut his own throat.

The President quickly and forcefully nods his head, and sets down his coffee cup, "Well...I'm glad you didn't try to deny knowledge of it, James, thank you. Plausible deniability. History's heard of that phrase far too often." He looks over to his Chief of Staff. "Frankly..." the President pauses, as if trying to come up with the right words, "Frankly, it's a load of crap."

Congressman Lopez feels panic rapidly crawling over him. He looks over at Senator Thurston who has a smug smile on his face, as if unfazed by the comment. Thurston sits up, slapping his hands in his lap gently, as if he is about to give a lecture. The President puts up his hand to clearly say, 'don't even try it.'

"I know what's been going on, and I know every mission Jones has been sent on by the two of you, with help from Waxman at the CIA." The President's voice raises a level, "And now Jones is missing, presumed grabbed by a foreign government." His voice grows even louder, "Right here in the United States! Good lord, this is unacceptable, gentlemen. Even if we get him back alive, I can't retaliate, officially. What would I say? I would have to admit that a CIA asset conducted covert actions in foreign countries, killing people, and blowing-up government buildings." Mitchell's voice level noticeably increases again, "There would be international outrage and some of those countries might feel the need to respond in-kind." The President pauses...a long pause. "I understand why you did it, and that's why you're not in handcuffs already, but *how* you did it, that's unfortunate. Do you have any idea how this now affects our international policy?" He looks at the two men, not really waiting for, nor wanting, an answer.

"I think we can manage the situation, Sir–" Thurston again attempts. The President interrupts.

"We? We? Absolutely not, James. There never was any 'we', and there is no 'we' now. You both are out. The Animus Project is finished. In fact, it never happened." Pointing at the men with the pencil he'd been holding, he nearly shouts, "You two are to have nothing more to do with Isaac Jones. I don't even want either of you to make contact with Waxman outside of budget or oversight hearings. Do you understand me?"

"Mr. President!" Thurston blurts-out.

"I'm serious, James. If you attempt to continue in this, or if I even get wind that you've mentioned the name 'Isaac Jones,' I'll have the DOJ so far up your butt it'll make a colonoscopy feel like Christmas morning! Now, I think we're done here. Mr. Harrison will show you out. Thank you, gentlemen."

The two men slowly get up and Harrison escorts them to the door, leaving them to be shown out by the President's secretary. He closes the door, sits back down, and says, "I think that went well," slyly smirking.

President Mitchell snaps the pencil in half, points to the door through which both men just left, and says to his Chief of Staff, "That's the type of American government that no longer works, Gio. And I *will* change it."

SOMEWHERE ABOVE THE NORTH PACIFIC OCEAN

Oliver Riley and his men hold their long-range binoculars up to their eyes. Riley pushes a button on the side of his flight helmet and speaks into the mic, "Crickey! Over there," he says, pointing out his side of the chopper. Without the binoculars, the view just looks like ocean waves cresting in the wind, but the long-range optical reveals a large cargo ship with a red stripe. "Not too close," he tells the pilot.

"Sir, you have a call from the mainland," the pilot tells him.

"Patch it in. Riley here," he says.

"Oliver, it's Elliot. We just landed. How far out are you?"

The pilot, who is also monitoring the call, holds-up his fingers, making out: 1-6-0-0.

"About 1600 kilometers off the coast. We found the ship! It looks pretty quiet, but we're not very close, so it's hard to say what's going on down there. They're still moving dog ass slow."

"Ok, come get us," Warren says.

"Do you think we should check it out first?"

"No, you might spook them and if you get into a fire fight you're going to need help, and I want to be there."

"From the size of that ship I think we could use the extra hands. That Bertha is huge. Let's hope it's not fully-staffed.

We're on our way," Riley says, indicating to the pilot they need to return to base.

Chapter 22

Blood drips from a forehead wound, down into his eyes, causing them both to intermittently sting. Isaac Jones is back in the holding cell tied to the same metal chair. His blood drips. The men have been taking turns beating him. He doesn't know how long he's been back in the chair; time seems to be moving in slow motion. The blood keeps dripping. After a few more blows to the head, the men leave the room, he's alone. All he can think of is Yon, as he does, a large lump in his throat develops. *Damn!* He screams in his head. Jones isn't one to dwell on regrets. He lives for the moment; the past is the past, and it can't be changed. *If you don't like what happened in the past, do better in the future*, is what he tells himself when moments of regret creep into his mind. Today, though, all he has is regret when it comes to what just happened to Yon. He knows she's a good swimmer, but they're in the middle of an ice-cold ocean, and her bleeding arm is bound to attract sharks. He can't think of any outcome that has a good ending for her.

He regrets not spending more time with Yon when he had the chance. Earlier today, when he asked her to come back to the States, he was planning on telling her that he loves her and wants her to move to the States with him. Though out of character for him to make such a commitment when life is such a rollercoaster, he is sure of his love for her. Now she's gone. His tears mingle with his dripping blood, slowly run down his nearly-broken cheekbones. Then his face changes, becoming angry. His eyes turn dark, and clinching his fists tight, he lets out a growl that echoes throughout the empty, metal room.

The door opens with a heavy thud as it hits the wall. Two men step inside and shut the door behind them. Jones looks up and sees Soju's brother, but can't make out the second one, who stays back in the shadows.

"Mr. Jones, you're not happy with our accommodations?" the Korean asks.

Jones pauses, lifts up his head, and looks through the tangled mix of bloody, wet hair, and says very naturally, "Untie me and I'll show you how happy I am."

"I think not. But I have someone here who wants to meet you."

The Korean turns and looks at the man in the shadows. He motions to the figure to step into the light.

"Mr. Jones, meet Comrade Brycekov," he pauses for sick, dramatic effect. "I think you know each other, *no*?"

As Brycekov moves into the light, Jones recognizes him immediately. He's the only one who got away in London during the Reagan connection mission. He also knows Brycekov was the one in Germany who almost persuaded his son, Michael, to martyr himself with a suicide vest, and kill everyone else around him.

Jones clenches his fists tightly and continues struggling to free himself from the chair. But the bindings don't budge, and instead dig into his skin with each attempt to break free. The white plastic is now crimson red. Jones glares at both men with rage.

"You're surprised to see me, I can tell," Brycekov says.

Jones just looks at him with eyes that clearly say, *what do you want?*

"I do not want anything," he pauses. "But then again, maybe I do. Maybe I want tickets! I know what my new friend here is planning to do with you and I simply didn't want to miss the show. So, when he invited me to come and watch, I thought it would not only be an opportunity to see my new friend face-to-face, but to see you face your death."

Jones laughs out loud, "North Korea and Russia working together, what a match made in hell."

"Our countries work together all the time, Mr. Jones. We have mutual respect for each other," replies Brycekov with a big smile. "And regarding Hell, well, simply let us know if that's correct, once we send *you* there." Brycekov and the Korean both laugh.

"That's the funny thing. It's like a bad comedy show," Jones manages to say quietly as his strength ebbs and flows. "Two of the most untrustworthy countries in the world trusting each other. Really?" Jones asks Brycekov.

"But, of course! If I did not, I wouldn't be on his ship, now would I?"

A mix of renewed energy joins an immediate awareness of the need to keep them talking to him, allowing each question to lengthen his life. Jones continues, "Wow, I'm sure they're taking odds in Vegas on how short this love affair will last. I must say I'm surprised. I mean, look at him," Jones pauses. Brycekov looks from him to the North Korean, who is looking at Jones. "He's the second ugliest North Korean I've ever seen. The first was his one-eyed brother…the one Yon and I s'mored."

"S'mored?" asks Brycekov, as the Korean moves back into the conversation with an equally unclear expression on his face. "What means, 's'mored'?" Brycekov says, as a quick follow-up.

"It's a little American tradition of torching a marshmallow…" Jones smiles, knowing he's just pushed the right button.

The North Korean screams at the top of his lungs and lunges at Jones, punching him in the jaw. Spit and blood fly from Jones' mouth.

Jones spits onto the floor and looks back at the big North Korean with a smile. He got under his skin, exactly what he wanted.

"I am going to enjoy killing you, Mr. Jones," the North Korean says.

Jones ignores the statement and looks back to Brycekov, "Who's Common?"

The question takes Brycekov off-guard.

"You heard me. Who's Common? I know you and Poloski were working together on the Reagan bombings, and he told me you were working for someone named Common. So, if I'm going to die anyway, why not tell me?"

The North Korean looks at Brycekov, "What's he talking about?"

Brycekov lifts his hand to his chin and scratches the stubble, considering his next move. Finally, he turns to the North Korean and says, "My friend, would you mind if I have a couple of minutes alone with Mr. Jones before you kill him?"

SOMEWHERE ABOVE THE NORTH PACIFIC OCEAN

Riley's chopper is speeding back toward the last location they saw the ship. On board now are Riley's Ranger recruits, along with Warren and Chase.

Twenty-five minutes prior, Warren had tried to get Chase to stay with Henry on the jet, but Chase refused, saying, "I was kicking butt and taking names while you were still sucking your thumb, you macho, British, dung-heap. *Let's go!*"

Warren laughed and said, "Wow, for a minister, you *do* have some fight left in you. Good, we might just need it. Punches and prayers, well, that's a new combo for me. Indeed, let's go," he said as he slapped Chase on the back with affection as they both boarded the chopper.

As they grabbed their seats, Chase looked-over the gear on-board and locked his focus on one of the Ranger recruits holding an AK-47. Looking over to Riley, Chase said, "I want one of those."

Riley looked at Warren and chuckled with satisfaction. "That-a-boy, Pops! Give him one of those pee-shooters! We have one in 'Baptist Brown', I believe," Warren said with a big grin, while slapping Riley on the back.

Chapter 23

In the Oval Office, Chief of Staff Harrison is hanging-up from a call with Ms. Stella. "Keep us updated, please," he tells her, and sets the phone in its carriage.

The President is at his desk and Harrison is seated on the couch. "They spotted the ship and are en route after picking up the other members of the team. The ship seems quiet, and is still navigating slowly. They should intercept it within the hour," Harrison briefs the President.

"Do they have enough manpower?"

"Well, between Warren, Riley, and Chase, they have some pretty lethal fighters. But they also picked up a chopper outfitted with two Rangers and 50k automatic fire. I think they might be a little light, but that's how they wanted it. We'll just have to trust them." Gio pauses, and then continues, "There are those on the team who won't admit it, but Warren says he doesn't expect to find Jones alive. Either way, the smaller the unit, the better. You know they're going to kill everyone on board, whether Jones is alive or not, right?"

"Yes, I do," the President replies.

"And you're good with that?"

"I'm perfectly fine with it, Gio. These men entered our country, kidnapped a CIA covert asset, and fled. I won't ignore something like that. All our enemies need to know that we will respond when challenged. I know years of inaction have left many terrorists, and some countries, wondering if we will still 'have it.' I'm telling you right now, we do!"

"I understand, Sir," Geo acknowledges.

"Do you agree?" the President asks.

"I do."

"Good."

"May I ask you one question, Mr. President?"

"Of course."

"When the Senator and Congressman were here, Thurston brought-up 'plausible deniability.' I know we've discussed this previously, but I've been wondering, assuming Jones returns alive and is still in good enough shape to continue," Harrison pauses, looking over his reading glasses at the President. "Perhaps we should reconsider how much you're involved."

"We've been over this. I'm the Commander in Chief, and I should be approving covert operations. Not all of them, but the special ones. When I say 'special,' I'm talking about the ones that could cause international outrage or a special hearing at the U.N...the ones that Jones seems to have a unique flair for."

"I understand, but what you call 'special' others might call illegal or, at the least, politically damaging. I would hate for a POTUS-approved black op to go wrong and derail your chance for a second term. That's all."

"Nonsense," the President says without hesitation, then smiles and says, "Gio, you are a good man, and you're always looking out for my best political interests. That ends today. Just as I told Lopez and Thurston: we do what's right for the nation. Period."

Harrison nods, "Yes, Mr. President."

NORTH PACIFIC OCEAN

Brycekov drags a heavy metal chair across the dusty floor and sits directly in front of Jones. Wiping his hands on his pant legs, Brycekov sighs and says, "What a dump, this place is filthy." He raises his chin in the air and closes his eyes, as if daydreaming. "I like the best of what life has to offer. I love the taste of a fine wine, taking a bite out of a perfectly prepared steak in a fine restaurant, an elegant hotel suite, and the fragrance of expensive perfume on a beautiful woman wearing nothing but diamonds."

He stops, opens his eyes, and looks directly into Jones' eyes. He breathes-in deep, and the exhales with each word, "Mother Russia was supposed to be the crown of all the jewels in the world."

He takes another breath. "Then your President Reagan came along and ruined it," shaking his head slowly. "Gorbachev didn't have the stomach to take him on. He halfheartedly tried, and failed. Once we realized he was going to lose the Cold War, we attempted a coup, but he foiled our plans. Well, it's time for my country to find its glory again. Too bad you won't be around to see it. But, enough about that. How about you? What do you find best out of life?"

Jones stares into Brycekov's dark eyes. This man makes him sick to his stomach. Initially, he thought he wanted to spit in his face, but instead pauses, deciding against it. "What do I find the best out of life? Well, you might be surprised to know that we share similar appreciation for some things. Love of nation, love of family." Jones pauses, considers, and then decides to go ahead. He calmly tells him, "The thing I like the most is looking evil directly in the eye and stopping it by sending men like you directly to hell. And have no doubt, there is a special set of chains waiting for you in hell."

Brycekov diverts his eyes, looking down with a slight grin, "You are a hard man. And you are mourning the loss of your friend, so I understand your hostility. But here you seem to be the only one whose hands are bound."

Jones changes directions, as he's been trained to do, "Who's Common?"

Brycekov looks up from the floor, "That is a tricky question, without an easy answer."

"Well, it seems we have nothing but time," Jones replies.

"No, your time is about up. But, I will tell you the question should not be 'who,' but rather 'what.'"

"How so?"

"COMMON is not a person, Mr. Jones."

A look of confusion sets in on Jones' face. "What are you talking about?"

"I've told you too much already. It's of no consequence to you. Just know that when we are finished, the United States will suffer much like my country suffered after the Cold War."

Jones decides he has nothing to lose and goes for the jugular, "You're crazy, aren't you? I mean, actually insane. You're a small, filthy, little piranha. You dream of living like a king, but you will always be the jester, just like your President Putin, you whack-job!"

The insults worked, and seem to enrage Brycekov. Standing up violently, Brycekov places his handgun directly into Jones' left temple, and shouts "And you are a dead man!"

Jones closes his eyes and waits for the shot. When a shot rings out, he flinches even though he's expecting it. There's no sting of a bullet. He hears a thud in front of him and slowly opens his eyes. There, lying on the dusty floor, is Brycekov, face-down with a bullet hole in the back of his head.

Jones senses movement from the shadows off to his side. Confused, he calls-out, "Who's there?"

A man steps out of the shadows toward him holding a foreign handgun. He's wearing a long, dark coat, and a dark fedora hat. He kicks Brycekov's gun away from his limp hand. He puts away his own weapon, and takes out a military knife. He flips it open and cuts-off Jones' binds, freeing his hands and feet.

Jones stands up. The two men are about the same height. Jones recognizes the familiar face beneath the hat. "Ackerley?"

The man smiles back at Jones.

176

Chapter 24

McBride did as suggested by the President's Chief of Staff, and went home for the day. He wasn't sure what was going on and wanted to be free to find-out. He called Senator Heart's office and was told she was unavailable. He then tries Brycekov on the cell but gets no answer. Taking a sip of his Crown-Royal over ice, he grabs the center of his tie and pulls it, releasing the knot, and pulls it off, throwing it across the room.

Could all my hard work be for nothing? he wonders. He truly believes he's the best person to run the CIA. If sacrificing Jones to the North Koreans was the price to pay, so be it. To him, Jones is a war criminal. *The ends do justify the means, in many cases,* he assures himself. *Did I commit treason?* he wonders nervously. He honestly hadn't considered the legal consequences. He knew that should anyone find out that he gave Jones' location to a foreign source, a lot of heat would be released against him. But Senator Heart supports him, so he decided to give the information, *was that wrong?*

He now realizes he *did* commit a crime...*A crime that could be distorted to look like treason, he* panics. *No!* he thinks to himself. *What I did was right for the future of the Agency, and America. We can't have a hotshot like Jones running around the world using the vast resources of the United*

States Government, committing torture and murder. That's not the way this country should operate, he thinks to himself, but only half-believing what he's telling himself. *But, if the President finds-out, I'm screwed!*

He takes another sip from his drink. *What should I do? I would have to disappear...permanently!*

He's deep in fearful thought. *But the President does not know...*

He picks up his phone and dials. "Mr. McBride's office," Hillary answers.

"Hillary, is anyone looking for me?" he asks.

"No, Sir. It's been quiet since you left."

He is relieved. "Alright, I won't be back in today, and I might be taking tomorrow off, too."

"Not feeling well, Sir?"

"I think I'm coming down with something. I'll let you know tomorrow. Anything new on the Jones issue?"

"Haven't heard a thing," she responds.

McBride hangs-up and sits back in his chair, finishing off his drink. "But the President does NOT know..." he says out loud to no one.

WASHINGTON, D.C.

Senator Thurston is on a videoconference with Congressman Lopez.

"Who does he think he is, telling us to butt-out and to close Animus down?" Thurston yells.

"You're kidding, right? He's the frickin' President of the United States, James!"

"Big deal! I was walking the halls of the Capitol before he graduated from high school."

"I warned you that if we continued, something like this might happen. The President gave us strict orders. *It's over.* Do you want this to go public? He could torch both of our butts. Can you imagine what an oversight committee hearing could do to our reputations and careers? We'd be finished *and* could end up in prison."

"That's never going to happen. He's bluffing, and I think he's underestimating how much pull I have on the Hill, Raul."

"You do what you want, but I'm out. Don't ever call me about it again. I know nothing. I've never heard of Animus, and don't know who Isaac Jones is. Understand?"

"Oh, don't be such a wuss. This is a bump in the road."

"The man still has three years left as President and could easily get another term. I'm washing my hands of it. Honestly, I never really wanted to be involved in the first place. Take my advice and do as I'm doing, or things could get really bad for you. Good-bye, Senator."

The Senator's monitor goes black as Lopez ends the conference, and Thurston sits back in his large, oversized chair. "Coward," he says out loud, knowing the Animus Project was never about revenge or protecting America.

For him, it was always about power.

Power to manipulate governments around the world and use Jones to get done what Congress and even the President don't have the stomach for.

Power to take the fight to the enemy without all the Washington, D.C. politically-correct red tape.

Power to make split-second decisions without first having to take a poll to see if the American people approve or not. *The American people are fickle. They change opinion on a dime. The world doesn't wait for the polls to continue spinning on its access. It continues to spin, regardless of the politically-correct mantra of the hour*, he thinks to himself.

Ultimately, it's the power to make the hard decisions in the shadows, out of the spotlight.

Like an addiction, once they started sending Jones out, all Thurston could think of was what to do next.

He liked the feeling. No, he *loved* the feeling.

The way the Senator sees it, for President Mitchell to attempt to take it from him, after all the good they've done, that shows him just how foolish this young President really is. And he refuses to stand for it.

He begins making plans.

NORTH PACIFIC OCEAN

"Ackerley?" Jones asks again, rubbing his newly-freed, blood-covered wrists. Jones knows this man as "Abbot Ackerley" from the North Korea mission. Jones and Yon had posed undercover as reporters to witness North Korea's latest missile launch. In reality, they were independently there to take-out the drone and missile control room. Ackerley was with them, as a reporter for The Guardian Newspaper in London, or so Jones thought.

"You can now call me 'Mr. Hill,'" the man says, picking-up Brycekov's gun, handing it to Jones. "I'm quite certain you know how to use this."

Jones is taken by surprise. In North Korea, Jones had introduced himself to Ackerley as "Mr. Nugent." "You know who I am?"

"I do, and we have to move quickly," Hill says, moving toward the door.

Jones doesn't budge, "Wait, who *exactly* are you?"

"Let's just say our common interests have collided. Brycekov needed to be eliminated and I prefer you to be alive."

"Our common interests?" There's that word again.

Hill turns and faces Jones. "That's right."

"You know what COMMON is, don't you?" Jones asks.

"Mr. Jones, right now we need to get you off this boat. The rest will come later."

"How did you find me?"

"Oh, so many bloody questions!"

Hill moves toward the door, "Right now some of your friends are about to land on this boat and are expecting a fight. It's in both of our best interests that there be no fight. My men have taken care of the North Koreans, and now Brycekov and his men are dead. The only people still alive on this ship are you and me. My men have placed chargers in the hull of this ship. It will be at the bottom of the ocean in less than fifteen minutes. We need to move. Step it up, cowboy!"

Hill opens the door and steps over two North Korean soldiers as he exits. Jones follows. "Up there, go right. The chopper should be landing soon. I'm going the other way to my transport. It's been good seeing you, Jones. I'm delighted you're still alive." Hill turns away and quickly leaves Jones standing alone, watching him disappear.

"What-in-the-hell?" he says to himself.

Jones isn't sure if what Hill just told him about all the threats being eliminated is true or not. He puts the gun up in front of him and slowly ascends the stairs to the opening of the deck. He scans, it's clear. He proceeds to the open area, looking up for the friends Hill said are on their way. He hears a chopper engine start and then sees it lift off the deck. It ascends quickly and disappears in a flash.

Then he hears another chopper coming in from the opposite direction. It appears to be attempting to give chase to Hill's chopper.

Jones holds up both arms and waves wildly. The arriving chopper slows and moves back in his direction, coming in for a landing. Jones releases a soul-deep sigh. It's over, he says to himself.

As the chopper lands, Riley, his men, Warren and Chase all jump out of the aircraft with their automatic rifles up, scanning for threats.

Warren runs to Jones. "Are you alright, old chap?"

"Man, am I glad to see you!" Jones says as he grabs Warren in a bear hug.

"Slow down there, Romeo. Let's clear this ship before you get all sentimental."

"Don't worry. All dead, it's just me," Jones tells him.

"That chopper?" Warren asks, pointing to the sky.

"Friendly, and this ship is rigged to sink in less than ten minutes."

"Yon?"

Jones looks down at the deck, without answering, and shakes his head.

"Damn, I'm sorry. Let's get you home." Warren puts an arm around his friend's shoulder and raises his other arm. With his index finger pointed up, he moves it in a circular motion, telling the others to load up.

Chapter 25

Jones and Warren jump into the chopper. The other men are already seated. Jones sits in the center seat and Warren straps him in. As the chopper lifts off, Jones lets out a deep sigh of relief. Riley scoots in next to him on the left, wearing a flight helmet, and slaps Jones' knee. He straps a flight helmet on Jones and pushes the audio button on the side.

"Great to have you back, mate," Riley says.

"Thanks. Are they your cousins?" Jones asks, pointing to the three men seated across from him.

"Nope, Yank's. Those two are courtesy of the Army Ranger battalion in Alaska. Being a former Ranger yourself I figured you wouldn't mind. Meet Tom…and Jerry," Riley smiles.

Jones nods his head, understanding, "No real names on this mission, huh? Glad to meet you both; I'm–"

"Tom" interrupts, "No need, Sir. We know who you are and we're glad you made it."

"As am I," the third man joins-in, taking off his flight helmet so Jones can see his face. He smiles wide, and puts his helmet back on so he could hear Jones over the noise.

"Eldon?! What are YOU doing here?" Jones asks his neighbor. "How? Why?" Jones looks over at Riley, who just shrugs his shoulders.

Jones looks over at Warren, "It wasn't my idea, Jonesy. Apparently, the top brass needed a chaplain," Warren says with a smirk.

Jones looks back to Eldon, who says, "It's a long story, son. I've been praying for your safe return."

"I've been doing a lot of praying myself," Jones says smiling.

"And what did you pray for?" Chase asks over the intercom, all ears listening.

Jones thinks for a moment, "I prayed that I would live to see another day and..." he pauses, his eyes welling up with tears, "I prayed that Yon made it to heaven."

"I'm sorry for your loss, she was a wonderful lady. When I prayed for you, I asked the Lord that you not be frightened or dismayed. And for you to know that God is with you wherever you go."

"Thank you." Jones stays quiet for just a little longer, gaining his composure. "Now, what are you doing here?"

"I'll fill you in when we get to the plane. A lot of people are very worried about you and will be glad to hear you're alright."

"I'm just glad it's over," Jones says.

"Over?" Warren reacts, and then speaks into the microphone, "As I once said to a certain, charming, young lass in Brussels, whose 'business,' shall we say, was on the top floor of a rather shady section of town, This is far from over, far from over."

SOMEWHERE ABOVE THE NORTH PACIFIC OCEAN

From his own chopper, Mr. Hill is on a phone uplink with Dohoyn Park. "Brycekov is dead, and the American is on his way home."

There was a slight, yet meaningful pause, "I told you to bring Brycekov back alive."

"Couldn't happen that way. He was about to kill the American," Hill responds.

"This is highly concerning, Mr. Hill. How am I supposed to explain this to the other members?" Park asks with an officially irritated tone.

"You don't. I'll explain when I return. Just keep your trousers on. I'll be back as soon as I can."

"You're not a senior member, Mr. Hill. For you to–"

Mr. Hill interrupts. "I do know protocol but this is about respecting the rules of membership in our organization. What Brycekov did could have put us *all* in jeopardy."

"I agree. Participating in the kidnapping of the American was far out of bounds and should never have happened," Park affirms.

"Brycekov killed the South Korean, too," Hill adds.

"Unfortunate."

"It bloody well is, not to mention that whole Reagan fiasco. Brycekov was involved in that, too."

The line goes quiet. Hill waits for Park to answer, then it hits him, "You knew about the Reagan attacks, didn't you?"

Again, no answer.

"Bloody Hell! *You did!* Did you know about Jones being grabbed in America, too?"

"No, I did *not* know about that. It was not a sanctioned mission. Brycekov acted on his own, outside of the group."

"Why wasn't I told about Brycekov's Reagan missions? What happened to our mandate about 'not being directly involved'? We give information to move the chess pieces, but don't touch the pieces on the board?" Hill's voice is getting uncharacteristically louder.

"I didn't tell you because you're the American's contact. You might have been conflicted, knowing we were supplying the Americans with information on action *we* were actually directly responsible for," Park replies.

"'Conflicted'? Don't be daft. I've never been conflicted about anything we do when it's the right thing. What I find devilishly wretched is you misleading our own members. We debate and vote if there's dissent. What's happened to our mandate and rules of operation? You and whoever else knew what was really going on are in violation or our own rules; rules that have been honored for decades. I don't understand. What possible benefit could the Reagan mission have gained us?"

"That's not your concern. Just return here and we'll sort it out."

Hill disconnects the line and curses out loud.

Chapter 26

The chopper lands in Alaska about 50 yards from the waiting CIA jet. As the men exit the chopper, Jones stops to thank the pilots, as well as "Tom and Jerry." As his boots hit the tarmac, the chopper rises again from the ground to return to base.

"How are you feeling?" Warren asks Jones.

"I'm hungry," Jones answers, as they walk toward the jet. Riley and Chase follow close behind.

The cabin door is open and the stairs are down. Hearing the chopper arrive, Henry walks from the galley to the cabin door; he looks down at the arriving men. He strains to see his frequent passenger while he silently prays that Jones' body isn't on a stretcher. Then, he recognizes the unique swagger. A big smile stretches across his face, *the old dog lives to fight another day*, he says to himself.

"This is as far as I go, Yank," Riley tells Jones before they arrive at the plane stairs. "I've still got work to do here."

"What? Come on - come with us. Take a few days off and spend them in America. I've gotta free plane ride," Jones says nodding toward the jet. Henry is now standing at the bottom of the stairs and waves to Jones. Jones gives a quick wave back, feeling a little uncomfortable with his status. This is new to him. He's never been the victim of an incident. He's the one who either causes the incidents or cleans them up. He doesn't feel comfortable having people fawn over him like a helpless child.

"No can do," says Riley, pulling Jones back from his thoughts. "I was working when I had to come and save your butt. Honestly, I think you purposely do these kind of things to test me, and see if I'll show up," Riley adds with a smile.

"No test. I already knew you'd show up. You're a good friend. Thanks, man!"

Riley holds out his hand for a shake. Ignoring the hand Jones pulls him in by the shoulders and gives him a hug. Both men slap each other's back with force, to say what they already know.

"Thanks, again," Jones says, releasing his friend.

"Anytime. You find out who's behind this and take care of it. I don't want to have to save you again."

"You got it."

"Oh, I almost forgot," Riley says, digging into his front pocket. He pulls out Jones' St. Michael pendant and gold chain, handing it to him. "Lose something?"

Jones smiles, while taking it. "No, it was right where I wanted it to be. Thanks."

Warren gives Riley a hug goodbye and says, "Thanks, you bastard cousin. Couldn't have done it without you."

Riley laughs and flips-off the Englishman, turns and walks over to Chase, still chuckling. Chase and Riley shake hands, and Riley jumps into a waiting jeep.

"Hi, Henry," Jones says, as he reaches the plane.

"I'm glad you're back, Sir," Henry responds.

"Thanks, buddy. I see you still need a haircut." Jones smiles and slaps him on the arm, taking the stairs, with Warren and Chase following.

The men plop into the first three front rows. Jones sits next to the window in his row. Warren sits across the aisle from him, and Chase sits in the next row behind Warren. The stairs are pulled-up, and the cabin door is shut and secured for takeoff.

"Henry, we need food, lots of food, dear boy," Warren commands as the jet taxies the runway and quickly takes to the sky.

Henry brings each man a bottle of water. "Will burgers and fries do?" he asks.

"That would be perfect," Jones answers. "Do you have a laptop with the encrypted video conference program on it?"

"I think so. Anything else?" Henry asks.

Jones nods, "I need Dragula, and loud." Henry nods and returns to the galley.

Jones then turns and looks at Warren. "I don't know exactly how you found me, or how you got dragged into this, but thanks, Elliot."

"There are a lot of people in on this, but my involvement came from your pretty flower, Stella, back at Langley, pushing me onto Waxman and the President."

"Stella called you in?"

Warren nods.

"The President? Of the United States?" Jones asks, surprised.

"No, the President of Uranus! Yes, the President of the United States you big oaf."

"That sounds like trouble," Jones mumbles.

"It sounds like he was concerned about you, and he personally authorized this mission."

"Seriously? I didn't know he even knew I existed."

"Yup. But I think he only recently got apprised of who you are and what you've been doing," Warren adds with a frown.

"That could be bad," Jones replies, then looks a row back at Chase. "And you," he says, standing up and moving to the seat across the aisle from his neighbor, "What in the world are you doing here?"

While Jones talks to Chase, "Dragula" by Rob Zombie begins to fill the cabin.

> *"Dig through the ditches*
> *And burn through the witches*
> *I slam in the back of my*

Dragula!"

Warren gets up, and finds Henry preparing the food with a sour look on his face. "What?" Warren asks.

"This song."

"What about it?"

"He only has me play it when he's *really* pissed."

THE WHITE HOUSE

Former FBI Director Ethan Christensen is again seated on the couch in the Oval Office. President Mitchell and Chief of Staff Harrison are in the two leather chairs to his right. On the coffee table in front of them is a videoconference monitor with Deputy Director Waxman's face in the middle of the screen.

"I know you're busy, Steven," the President tells Waxman, "but Ethan says he has some important information that you need to hear. But, first give us an update on the Jones mission."

"Riley picked up Warren and Chase a while ago and they, along with two Army Rangers from Fort Richardson, are on a chopper now in route to a ship they think might be the one we're looking for."

"Alright. I hope getting the Brits and Australians involved in this doesn't backfire on us," the President responds.

"I've talked to both of the Ambassadors for Britain and Australia. They understand the sensitivity of this issue and support you and the mission, Sir," Waxman affirms.

"Very well. Now, Ethan, what do you have for us?" the President asks, looking from the computer monitor to the former CIA Director.

Christensen shifts forward, resting his elbows on his knees. "First off, I want to suggest that once I tell you what I've found out, that that we all keep calm."

"Ethan, just tell us," the President commands.

"I know who the mole inside the CIA is."

"Who?!" Waxman asks just below a yell.

Christensen pauses, knowing the firestorm he is about to ignite, and finally says, "Trent McBride."

"What?" the President says in disbelief, looking over at Chief of Staff Harrison who also looks concerned and surprised.

"How good is your intel?" Harrison asks.

"One hundred percent. Earlier today I heard a recording of McBride talking to one of the men responsible for grabbing Jones. It's him alright," Christensen confirms.

"Good Lord!" the President says, his face turning red with anger. "I want him arrested this instant!"

Christensen stands-up. "Mr. President, don't let your emotions get in the way of how this should be handled."

"My emotions?! He's a traitor to this country. It has to be dealt with immediately."

"So, what do you propose?" Christensen asks. "Arrest him? Mirandize him, and give him a lawyer? Then have a very public trial where Jones' and the missions are the top story in every newspaper and internet news page in the world?"

"He's right, Mr. President," Waxman adds, as the seriousness of what he's just learned about his boss sets in.

"What are you suggesting?" Harrison inquires.

"We do nothing, *for now*," Christensen answers.

"Do nothing?" the President responds incredulously.

"For now. Waxman can lock him out of all classified areas and mirror his computer to keep an eye on what he's doing while we decide how to proceed," Christensen says.

"I can do that," Waxman confirms.

"Where is he right now?" the President demands.

"I talked to him earlier and told him to take a few days off," Harrison says.

They overhear Waxman saying, "Stella, find-out where Trent McBride is. Quietly. Stella's checking," he tells the men in the Oval Office.

"Ethan, how did you get this information?" the President asks.

"I'm sorry Mr. President, I can't tell you."

The President's eyebrows rise. "You can't or won't?" he asks, looking Christensen deep in the eyes. Christensen looks back with eyes showing no intimidation by the President, nor even worry that he was denying the President's question inside the Oval Office.

"Mr. President, I've sat in this very room with four different Commanders in Chief, counting you. I have learned over the years that there are some things better kept near to the vest, even from you. I'm sorry, but I'm not going to tell you. You're just going to have to trust me that this information is accurate."

"I just can't believe it," the President says to no one directly. "Senator Heart suggested he be nominated as the new Director." He looks at Harrison, who almost imperceptibly shrugs his shoulders.

Waxman breaks-in, "Stella was told by Hillary that McBride went home for the day."

"Perfect. Here's what we do..." Christensen begins.

Chapter 27

"I'm waiting," Jones says calmly to Chase as Henry delivers the burgers.

Henry interrupts, "Mr. Jones, I have a laptop for you when you're ready, and Mr. Waxman is asking for an update. I haven't told him you're on-board yet."

"Don't, I'll call him in a minute. Thanks, Henry." Henry hands Jones the laptop and Jones looks back at Chase. "Now Eldon, if that's really your name, I have three questions," Jones counts off with his fingers. "Who are you? What are you? And what are you doing here?"

"I am so glad you're well, Isaac. I demanded that Waxman allow me to come with Mr. Warren to help. When I saw the men drag you out of your house and toss you into that van, I knew they were professionals...or most likely government assets."

"And how would you know that? Have you been playing me? Is everything you've told me a lie?" Jones asks more clinically than emotionally.

"Good heavens, no. My name *is* Eldon Chase. I do live in that house next to you. I became a pastor at my church after

I retired. My wife did pass away from cancer. Everything I've told you is the truth, Isaac. I simply didn't answer questions you never asked."

"Like?"

"You never asked me what I retired from, and I didn't feel the need to tell you."

"So tell me, Eldon, quit making me drag it out of you."

"The short version is, I was you, about thirty years ago."

Jones looks surprised. "You were CIA?"

"Yes."

"Counter terrorism?"

"Among other things."

"And now?"

Chase lets out a long sigh, "Now, I'm what's called a 'black location guardian'. I keep an eye on the assets when they're home, and I keep an eye on the location when the assets are in the field. I make sure the location is secure and evaluate the assets' mental status."

"You're kidding. You've been spying on me this whole time?" Jones asks in disbelief.

"Who better to spy on a spy, than a former spy?" Chase says through a toothy smile. "Problem is, now you know I'm keeping an eye on you. When those men grabbed you, I wasn't sure if you'd make it back alive. I wanted to come and help, even if it meant compromising my position. After all, the location's empty, now isn't it?"

Henry returns, "You haven't eaten anything," he says to Jones. "Mr. Waxman is getting impatient."

"Yeah, ok, Henry." Jones smirks at Eldon, picks up his plate and barks at Chase, like a friendly neighbor's dog, "We're not done discussing this. I have to make a call."

"Roger that. Go make your call. There are a lot of worried people waiting," Chase answers, shooing Jones away with both hands. "I need a nap anyway."

Jones returns to his seat with the laptop. Across from him, Warren puts the last bit of burger in his mouth and leans over, toward him, "Need some more Rob Zombie before you make that call? Perhaps we can get your elderly friend and your young friend to join us in the mosh pit later?" Warren chuckles at his clever twist of words, music and emotions.

"Up yours!" Jones laughs, "That's my *get focused* music. You being a snooty British snob wouldn't understand. You probably listen to Dusty Springfield when you want to get your thoughts clear," Jones shoots back.

Warren roars with his distinct laugh. "How did you know? Maybe 'I just don't know what to do with myself' should really be my theme song!"

"Fits perfectly. Now, if you don't mind, I need to make a call," Jones says, lifting up the screen of his laptop. "I was just held captive by some pretty nasty dudes, in case you don't remember?" he says scolding.

"Make your call, make your call, Mr. Important," Warren says looking toward the cabin, waving one hand in the air and yells, "Henry, cue-up some Dusty Springfield! I'm feeling aggressive and might just kick Mr. Jones' ass if I don't calm down," he looks back to Jones with a brash smile.

"You're a class act," Jones says, pressing the power button on the laptop. Suddenly over the speakers comes "Son of a Preacher Man" by Dusty Springfield. Jones looks up and says, "That's it! That-is-it, Henry, you're fired! And take me back to that ship! I'd rather be held captive by Russians than listen to this!"

Warren roars with laughter again, Henry pokes his head out with a smile.

"Henry, dear boy, you're alright!" Warren says, clapping. Jones takes a handful of French fries off his plate and throws them at him. Warren catches a fry in his mouth.

Jones logs into the encrypted video call program and clicks the link. He spots the green light emanating from his monitor, indicating his camera is now transmitting. Within seconds Ms. Stella's face appears on the screen.

"Isaac!" she nearly yells as she looks up, seeing his face on her monitor.

Jones notices that she appeared to be on the verge of tears, "Hey, beautiful."

"Are you all right?"

"I'm fine," he says, trying to give her a reassuring smile.

"I've…" she pauses, "…*we've* been dreadfully worried about you. Are you sure you're alright?"

"Yep, I'm fine." He pauses deeply, trying to say the next few words, "Yon didn't make it, Stella," he says, his eyes clouding instantly as he speaks.

Ms. Stella lifts both hands across her mouth, "Oh, no…that's so…terrible!"

After an equally long pause ensues, she says, "I'm so sorry."

Seeing Stella's emotion makes him pause. He focuses on pushing the emotions away, thinking to himself, *It's not time to grieve yet, I have to be strong and finish this.* He responds, "I'm just not sure how to process all of it yet. All I'm currently concentrating on is finding out who betrayed us."

"Isaac, when we lost you–"

"You didn't lose me. I'm here and I'm going to finish this. I'm sorry, but right now I just need to talk with Waxman, alright? We can talk when I get back."

"Alright," Stella agrees.

"Hey, Stella."

"Yes?"

"Thanks for being concerned," he says with a smile.

Ms. Stella nods through tears, as the screen goes black. Jones lets out a deep breath and Deputy Director Waxman's face appears on the screen, "Isaac, thank God!"

"Thanks for sending help."

"You know we don't leave anyone behind," Waxman says.

"Yeah, that's a nice motto, but considering my black status I wasn't so sure anyone would be coming," Jones replies.

Waxman smiles, "Had I not sent anyone, Stella would have gone herself! She was actually the one who called your friend, Warren, without even telling me. He was on a plane coming this way before I even knew what was going on. Sometimes I wonder who's really running the show around here, me or her."

Jones smiles back, nodding, "Well, thanks."

"Were they North Koreans, Isaac? The President is waiting for an update," Waxman says.

"I heard the President authorized my rescue personally. Since when do we get the White House involved?"

"Had no choice. McBride was trying to call the shots and I needed someone over his head. Needless to say, POTUS is anxious to meet you."

"I'm not sure what to make of that. When we started, I never imagined I'd ever interact with, let alone talk directly to, the President of the United States," Jones says.

"Well, get ready, because he knows who you are, and what we've been doing. He wants to talk *confidentially* with you when you get back. So, North Koreans?"

"I'm not sure exactly who ordered the grab. There were North Koreans and Russians involved, though," Jones tells Waxman.

"That's what Ethan thought, too," Waxman pauses. "And they had some inside help."

"What are you talking about?" Jones sits up quickly.

"I'll fill you in when you land. Just get some rest, alright?"

"They killed Yon, Steven," Jones says.

"I'm so sorry. I know how much she meant to you."

"You know I'm going to finish this, right?" Jones adds.

Waxman leans in and looks directly into the video camera lens, as though he were in the same room with Jones. "I'd expect nothing less."

Chapter 28

Trent McBride is on his way to a good drunk.

As he sits at his dining room table, he wonders how things went so far off track. One minute, he's about to be nominated as the next director of the CIA, and the next minute, the White House tells him to take a few days off, shutting him out of the Jones investigation.

It's not fair, he thinks. *I'm a patriot. I've done so much for this country.*

He reaches down and lifts his pant leg, removing from his sock a small piece of paper folded in a square-shaped envelope. He carefully opens one of the flaps, and squeezes the corners together pushing the envelope open wide. Carefully, he pores some of the contents out on the table, white crystals shine under the ceiling's light. He takes out his wallet and pulls out his visa card. He chops the crystals into a fine white powder. He then spreads the powder into even lines. He removes a $20 from his wallet and rolls it into a straw shape.

His eyes are bloodshot and wide, "I'm a patriot. I've done so much for this country!" he loudly says. "Ungrateful bastards!"

He lifts the makeshift currency straw to his nose and lowers his face. The powder is vacuumed quickly into his nose, one line for each nostril. His eyes water slightly as he taps the bill on the table knocking off any clinging residual powder.

Still talking out loud to himself, "I'm always there. Always available!"

He licks his right forefinger and runs it across the table, capturing all the powder left behind, and spreads it across his teeth and gums. He smiles as the instant tingling and numbing effect takes over.

McBride sniffs hard, sucking the powder from his nose cavity down into his throat, making it go numb and tingle, too. He smiles, feeling of every drug addict's euphoria, at the contradiction of vices in his body: the liquid downer and the powder upper. *I feel good.* He smiles and sits back, closing his eyes as all of the day's problems begin to drift away.

In time, his cell phone rings, startling him from his pseudo-slumber. He looks at the screen, it reads, "Unknown."

Hesitantly, he answers, "Hello?"

Do-hoyn Park of COMMON responds. "Mr. McBride, we don't know each other, but we have mutual friends. Can you talk?"

"Who is this?"

"I would rather not say, this call is rather, sensitive in nature," Park answers.

"Is this some kind of joke?" McBride says, raising his voice, paranoia setting in again, *perhaps it's a setup*, his mind screams. "Goodbye, don't call me again."

His head is spinning from the drink and powder. He starts to lower the phone from his ear when the man says, "I know about Isaac Jones and your involvement. You might be in serious trouble."

McBride stops and takes a deep breath. He runs his tongue over his teeth subconsciously, "I'm listening."

"Is this line secure?" Park asks.

"It's a little late to ask that now isn't it? Yes, this phone is encrypted! How might I be in trouble?" Self-preservation is settling in.

"The North Koreans and Russians who grabbed Jones are all dead, and he's been rescued," Park simply states.

McBride's mouth falls wide open, "Rescued?! By who?"

"I don't have all that information but it's clear that you may have been compromised."

Beads of sweat form on McBride's forehead and his jaw jerks to the left and right nervously, "'May have,' what does that mean?"

"I don't know for sure…yet, but I thought you should know."

"I think I understand who you are, but why am I hearing this from you and not the other contact I usually talk to?"

"Because he's dead."

McBride's eyes become as dead as the disconnected line that now buzzes in his ear.

THE WHITE HOUSE

President Mitchell is talking to Deputy Director Waxman on his speaker phone in the Oval Office, "That is excellent news, Steven! Get him home, and I want to see him as soon as he's able."

"Yes, Sir. One more thing."

"Yes."

"The South Korean asset didn't make it. Jones was very close to her and is extremely upset."

"I understand. Tell him I'm sorry for his loss."

"It might be better if you tell him personally when you see him. Also, Sir, he'll expect to respond."

"How so?"

"He's a unique man. He'll want to use his unique skills. They've made it personal."

"Steven, I can't have—"

"Forgive me for interrupting, Mr. President. You must understand, a man like Jones won't just sit back and pretend this never happened. With him being grabbed and his close friend being murdered, he's not going to look the other way while politicians decide the best course of action."

"I am the Commander in Chief of the United States of America, Steven. He will heed my instructions."

Waxman pauses, "Of course, I understand, Mr. President. And this is exactly why the Oval Office has been kept out of our work from the beginning. It's ugly business and ugly decisions have to be made sometimes, decisions that could hurt politically. But that's what it takes to keep America safe, and what it takes for people like Jones to be willing to get down in the dirt. If you don't let him," Waxman pauses again, "if you don't let *us* do our work, you might as well close us down and forget you ever heard the name Isaac Jones, because believe me when I tell you, he *will* respond, with or without your approval. And, if it's 'without', he'll respond, then disappear and we'll never see him again, which means we will have lost one of the most efficient assets this Agency has ever seen."

The President slowly considers what Waxman had just told him, and then replies, "I'll take it into consideration, Steven. Thank you, and I won't make any decision until I speak with Mr. Jones personally."

"I understand, Mr. President. Thank you."

"Steven, I appreciate straight talk from the man I want as the next CIA Director. I don't get a lot of that around here, and I need it, especially from the CIA."

"Thank you, Mr. President."

Chief of Staff Harrison bolts in to the Oval Office, "Sir, you need to see this," he says grabbing the TV remote control, pressing the power button.

The President looks up from his desk with a confused look. "I'm on the speaker phone with Steven Waxman."

"Good, you both need to see this!" Harrison points the remote at the bank of four TV monitors and they came to life, each on a different news channel: Fox News, CNN, MSNBC, and C-Span. C-Span is showing a house vote, but the other three are all covering the same story. The headlines read, "American CIA operative kidnapped in Idaho."

"Good Lord!" the President says as the full impact of the headlines settle in. He drops a pen from his hand onto the desk.

Harrison turns up the sound on one of the channels, catching the reporter in mid-sentence, *"...although neither the White House or the CIA have confirmed this story, we have it from reliable sources that a CIA agent was in what they call a 'black location' in the State of Idaho, and someone, perhaps a foreign government, infiltrated the location, grabbed the agent, and somehow, was able to deliver him away from American soil. Where this CIA agent is now, and if he is still alive, is unknown. For now, all the American government is saying is, 'No comment.' Back to you, George, in the studio."*

"How did they get the story?" demands the President.

"No idea, I was just as surprised as you are. Now, not only does the Press want to know, but your press secretary is walking around like a deer caught in the headlights, the DOJ is scrambling, and my phone has been ringing off the hook from members of Congress wanting to know what we know," Harrison says.

"Steven?" the President asks.

"I just turned it on. I have no idea." He pauses, "Perhaps McBride?"

"Or Senator Thurston," Harrison says.

The President looks up with a shocked expression. "He wouldn't dare!"

CAPITOL HILL - WASHINGTON, D.C.

Senator James Thurston is seated at his desk in his office at the United States Capitol Building, with a satisfied smile on his face. He's been watching the news, with approval. He leaked the story about twelve minutes ago, regarding Jones being snatched, to various selected media sources he could trust. *This President doesn't know who he's messing with*, he smugly thinks to himself.

He turns up the volume on the TV to a CNN anchor who is talking to a retired CIA employee. "*...if true, it is a very dark day for the CIA*," the man says. "*The fact that the White House and the CIA spokesperson have no comment is troubling, at best.*" The anchor then says, "*And on Capitol Hill, Members of Congress are just as concerned,*" the screen cuts away to a sound-bite of Republican Congressman Stan Huntsman, "*I don't know anything about this report, but if it's true, the CIA and the White House need to brief Congress immediately. If a foreign government has come onto American soil and kidnapped an American, an employee of the CIA, this could be considered an act of war that cannot go unanswered.*"

Thurston clicks the TV off, "Get yourself out of this one, young Mr. Mitchell."

Chapter 29

Isaac Jones is finally sleeping. He tosses and turns to the sound of the jet engines, trying to relax, after his video call with Waxman and Ms. Stella. He pushes the button that reclined his seat back and closes his eyes.

Eventually, he dreams of the day he brought Michael home the first time to his townhouse in Idaho, and the look on the young boy's face as he took in his new life. His dream then moves to one day before Michael went back to boarding school, how Michael had told him he missed his family yet never wanted to go back. Michael told him that he is now his family and thanked him for saving him. Michael gave him a hug and said, "Thanks, Dad." That was the first time Michael had ever called him by that tender name. An unexpected knot developed in his throat as he fought off happy tears and said, "You're welcome, little man."

Then the scenery in the dream morphs. Jones is now in swimming trunks, lying on the sand of a silvery white beach. It is an unfamiliar setting, and he doesn't recognize the location. The sky is cloudless and bright blue. He can feel the warm sunshine on his face and the smell of the ocean calming his senses. He watches the tide carelessly rush in and out over that glistening, silver sand with the sound of a lone seagull in the distance. He sees a margarita glass on the ground next to him with an equally brilliant white salt glued to the rim, sparkling in the sun. He smiles, relaxes, and closes his eyes as he takes in the warmth. The song "Summer" by War, starts playing in his head,

"Cause it's summer
Summer time is here
Yes, it's summer
My time of year."

In his dream, Jones opens his eyes, catching movement in the water. It is a woman standing knee-deep in the ocean. She has a towel wrapped around her head and another towel in her hands patting the wetness from her skin. He sits up on his towel, squinting his eyes, commanding them to focus on the image off in the distance. It is quite obviously a woman wearing a red bikini top and matching bottoms. Jones smiles taking in her lovely figure. She is thin but curvy, and it makes him smile. *Thin is fine but not too thin*, he thinks to himself in the dream. *The curves of a woman's body are a splendid gift from above.*

The bikini isn't overly revealing, more conservative in its covering, another trait Jones likes. He likes it when there is more left to the imagination than shown. Women who show too much skin appear desperate to him. Although many would think a woman would have to be confident in herself to show a lot of skin in public, to Jones it's the opposite: it actually reveals insecurity. A confident woman doesn't need to show skin to get attention; a confident woman's personality is much more appealing than a woman strutting around in over-revealing attire.

Jones takes in her bronze shoulders as her arms raise to pull on the towel on her head. As if she knows she is being watched, she starts to turn toward him. *Yon?* he thinks. As if in slow motion, the towel comes down, revealing a mane of blonde hair falling to her shoulders as she turns. Ms. Stella looks back at him. Making eye contact, she smiles and begins walking toward him.

Then Jones hears a man's voice say, "Mr. Jones, Mr. Jones."

He feels his shoulders being nudged. He opens his eyes from the dream, and sees Henry standing over him. "Henry?"

"We'll be landing soon."

"Alright, thanks," he says, wiping the sleep from his eyes, wishing he were still on his dream beach. "Is there time for a margarita?" he sleepily mumbles.

THE WHITE HOUSE

The President's spokesperson, Mark Ruben, looks much calmer than he really is. At the end of yesterday, he started getting inquiries about a CIA operative having been kidnapped out of a CIA black location in Idaho. He was taken completely off-guard. More concerning, however, was when he asked Chief of Staff Harrison if he knew anything about the story and was shut down hard. "The White House has no comment, Mark. Don't say another word until you hear from me."

"What *do* you know?" Ruben pressed.

"Not a word!" Harrison answered, walking away.

He left the White House that evening incredibly angry. *It's my job to deal with the Press. If I'm out of the loop, I can't do my job*, he thought.

This morning he's dressed in a smartly fitted charcoal suit and black tie. Ruben is almost forty, but looks younger and has on his signature black-framed glasses. He was hired as President Mitchell's spokesperson during the campaign and became the President's Senior Press Secretary shortly after the inauguration.

He arrived at his office purposefully early on this particular morning to beat the Press' arrival. He didn't want to field any more questions about this CIA issue until he has some answers.

He sits at his desk and dials his counterpart at the CIA, Julie Moore. Mark and Julie know each other well, they have worked together on numerous issues ensuring the CIA and White House are disseminating identical information. They both take their jobs seriously and make sure they never gave the impression that one hand doesn't know what the other is doing. Consistent messaging is the key, they were told by Chief of Staff Harrison, and they live by that rule. Julie had a similar day yesterday, so Mark isn't surprised she is in her office this early morning, too.

"This is Julie," she says, picking up her phone.

"Julie, it's Mark."

"Mark! What is going on?"

"I was hoping you would know."

"I'm being stonewalled here. My guess is they are deciding how to respond. What's strange is that they are keeping me out of the planning. They have *never* kept me out. I don't know what to think."

"What have they told you?" Mark asks.

"Nothing. Trent McBride has been my supervisor since the Director resigned and yesterday no one seems to know where he is either. I told his secretary, Hillary, it was imperative I speak with him and she said he was unavailable. I asked around and no one has seen him," she informs.

"Holy crap! You don't suppose McBride is the one whose missing do you?"

"I do find it strange that the story breaks at the same time McBride is missing."

"Keep digging, and I'll see what I can find out here. What time is your morning press briefing?"

"Nine, I'm thinking about canceling it."

"Same here. I'll call you at eight-thirty."

As Ruben hangs-up, the door to his office opens and Chief of Staff Harrison steps in. "Good morning, Mark."

Ruben is momentarily stunned. He uncharacteristically reaches down and turns on the recorder on his iPhone to record whatever is about to be said. It's a fluid and undetected movement.

Something's up, Harrison has never visited his office before. He always had Mark come to him. "Good morning, Sir."

"So, what exactly does the Press think they have?"

"Did you see the news last night and this morning?" Ruben asks.

"Yes, but I want to know what they are asking you."

"Pretty simple. They think a CIA employee was grabbed out of a black location in Idaho and want us to confirm the story, and what our response is."

"Where did they get a wild story like that?"

Ruben gets a curious look on his face. He hadn't expected such a cavalier response. Yesterday he was told harshly by Harrison only to say, "No comment."

"So, it's not true?" Ruben inquires.

"I can assure you that after a complete assessment of all CIA employees, none are missing."

"Alright, how about off-the-books employees or sub-contractors?" Ruben pries, knowing he will be getting the same probing by the Press at his briefing.

"Everyone is accounted for. I don't know where the Press gets their information, but the CIA isn't missing anyone," Harrison says calmly.

"And the Idaho connection? If the Press checks with local law enforcement, are they going to find anything? Do we have a black location in Idaho? Has one been compromised recently?"

"We do not currently have any operating black locations or safe houses in Idaho, and as far as the White House knows, there are no plans to have any. There may have been some in the past, but as far as the White House knows, there aren't any active. If the press wants more information on that, tell them to ask the CIA."

Ruben's brow furrows. "Just so I have this straight, the White House knows nothing about any missing CIA employee, and as far as we know, there are no black locations or safe houses in Idaho."

"That's right, keep it just that simple. Thanks, Mark." Harrison turns and walks out.

Chapter 30

Deputy Director Waxman and Stella are on a videoconference with President Mitchell.

"Stella had both Jones' and Chase's rentals cleaned-up and packed-out last night and told the rental company we're cancelling our lease."

"Can the lease be tracked back to the CIA?" the President asks.

"Not likely," Stella responds. "They were rented using a ghost account registered to a holding company in Florida. The trail should end there."

"And the local cops?"

"I talked to Chief Roe and county Sheriff Reynolds last night. They understand our situation, and agreed to silence. I suppose if the Press is unsatisfied with Mark's answers this morning, they could start digging around and find a local officer who might say there was a disturbance, but it shouldn't go much further," Waxman informs the President.

"Fine. And have you briefed State on what Julie can say?"

"I just talked to her, she's very bright. She knows we're keeping something from her, but she'll keep our talking points on message," Waxman assures the President.

"Very good work, you two. And, Jones?"

"They landed late last night. We put Chase, Warren and him in suites at the Hyatt under sterile names. I told Jones a car would pick him up at one-o'clock and bring him to the White House. Would you like me to attend the meeting?" Waxman asks, desiring to be in attendance, yet not wanting to sound like McBride.

"Not necessary. I think I would like some one-on-one time with Jones. Thank you, though."

Waxman relaxes, knowing that President Mitchell made no comparison.

THE WHITE HOUSE

The President's spokesperson, Mark Ruben, is in the Press Briefing Room for the morning briefing. His brown hair is pulled back, away from his perspiring and glistening forehead. He's prepared for a quick chat with "the vultures," his in-office name for the White House Press Pool.

"I have a short statement, then I will take a few questions," he says. "As far as the White House knows, there are no, I repeat, there are no CIA employees missing or suspected kidnapped. We do not know where your colleagues at the

New York Times and Washington Post received their information, but they are misinformed."

The room explodes into an uproar with reporters jumping to their feet, shouting questions, some with their hands raised, others just yelling.

Ruben holds up his arms motioning for the room to calm down. He then points to a reporter in the front row, "Andy?"

"You said, 'as far as the White House knows, there are no missing CIA employees.' Does that mean there could be missing agents, outside of your knowledge? And what about sub-contractors, or off-the-books assets?" the reporter asks.

"C'mon, Andy...my answers stand without any hair-splitting. We consulted with the CIA and they told us there are no missing employees, sub-contractors or otherwise, at this time. As far as what might be known outside of my knowledge," he pauses for dramatic effect, "you don't really think I would be able to answer about things I don't know about, do you?" Ruben replies with an almost condescending tone.

A female reporter standing next to Andy yells out, "Does the CIA have a safe house in Iowa?"

"Kris, seriously? Idaho. And that would be a question for the CIA, but as far as the White House knows, there are no active CIA locations in I-da-ho. Thank you." Ruben closes his notebook and leaves the podium to the shouts of more questions from the Press Pool.

CAPITOL HILL - WASHINGTON, D.C.

Congressman Lopez has been glued to the news all night and throughout the morning. He's shocked that word of Jones' kidnapping was leaked to the Press. His gut tells him Senator Thurston is the leak. He picks-up the phone and dials. Thurston's secretary answers and puts him through.

"Good morning, Raul, how are you this beautiful morning?" Thurston answers cheerfully.

"Did you do this?" the Congressman asks more calmly than he feels.

"Whatever are you talking about?"

"Did you leak to the Press about Jones?"

"You're darn tootin' I did!" Thurston bellows with a smile the size of the Potomac River.

"Why, James?"

Thurston responds with a slight giggle, "You know why. If that snot-nosed, green-under-the-collar President thinks he can shut ME out of my own project, he's mistaken! I was making laws and protecting this country while he was still breast feeding and sitting in diapers!"

"Do you have any idea what you've done?" Lopez asks.

A long pause silently muffles any remaining laughter from the senior Senator. Then, Thurston's attention is grabbed by a headline scrolling across the bottom of the TV screen,

"W.H. says no CIA employees are missing in response to report in New York Times and Washington Post."

"I have to go, Raul," he says, hanging-up the phone.

Lopez quickly dials another number: the White House switchboard. "Extension, please?" the warm female voice asks.

"Good Morning. This is Congressman Lopez. Could I have Chief of Staff Harrison, please?"

"Hold, please," the operator calmly replies, as the line goes to an elevator music rendition of the Bee Gees, "Staying Alive."

LANGLEY, VIRGINIA

Deputy Director Waxman is at his desk, reading the morning edition of the New York Times. For now, the safe-house attack story seems to have lost steam. His phone buzzes and Ms. Stella announces through the speaker, "I have Special Agent Jorden from the FBI on the line."

Waxman looks over from his newspaper to the phone, "FBI? What does he want?"

"No idea, he just asked for you," Stella answers.

"Tell him I'm occupied," Waxman tells her.

"This is his third call this morning. I've been putting him off."

Waxman knows Jorden well. They went to boot camp together and have drinks occasionally to keep in touch. They are friendly, but not friends.

"Fine, send the call," Waxman says. There's a click and the phone buzzes again, Waxman picks-up the receiver. "This is Waxman."

"Steven, I've been trying to reach you."

"Hi, Max, I heard. What's up?"

"The Director asked me if I knew anything about this Idaho issue. I told him I didn't have any information, but would reach out to you since we know each other."

"What issue in Idaho?" Waxman asks.

There is a pause on the line, as if Jorden wasn't expecting that answer, "Um, the story that's been all over cable news and in the newspapers about one of your men being kidnapped."

"Oh, that," Waxman says calmly. "I think we have been very clear that none of our people are missing and they must have gotten bad information."

"Nevertheless, I told him I would ask you about it."

"All right, now you've asked, and let me make myself very clear...the CIA is not missing any personnel."

"Steven, we've known each other a long time. Is that all I'm going to get?"

Waxman lets the question float on the air, without a need for a response.

Jorden continues, "Local law enforcement is telling us that there was an incident and the CIA took-over the investigation, then cleared-out early this morning. Needless to say, the Bureau is feeling left-out."

"The CIA doesn't have any black sites in Idaho, and even if we did, the FBI has no jurisdiction in a CIA black sight–"

Jorden interrupts, "If there was a crime at the site, the FBI does have jurisdiction. The CIA has no authority to investigate crimes in the Homeland."

"Max, none of our people are missing. That location is not CIA property, and if the FBI wants to enter, it's fine with me. You let the Bureau Director know that if he has a problem, to talk to the White House."

"The White House?"

"You heard me. Now, I'm in the middle of a rather busy morning. Let's grab a drink soon." Waxman hangs-up and flops back in his chair, he's feeling worn out.

These aren't the droids you're looking for,' pops into his mind, for no apparent reason.

Chapter 31

Mark Ruben is on the phone with CIA spokesperson Julie Moore, "I feel left out on this one. There's definitely more going on here," Ruben says.

"How do you know? Maybe it's like they say, bad info. It wouldn't be the first time the Press ran with a leak that was untrue."

"Because I'm being kept out of the loop. Harrison won't give me the President's schedule today. He had a full afternoon but it was scrubbed at the last minute. Apparently, he has people coming over for a high-level meeting."

"With whom?" Moore asks.

"No idea."

"All right. Let me know if you get any more information," she says, hanging-up.

Ruben shrugs as he, too, disconnects.

HYATT HOTEL, WASHINGTON, D.C.

Isaac Jones and Eldon Chase are having breakfast in the hotel restaurant. Jones is poking his fork at the last portion of his Eggs Benedict and Chase is polishing off a fruit platter.

"You seem down, Isaac. Want to talk about it?"

"I have to be honest, I'm not sure how to talk to you anymore. I thought you were my friend and come to find out you were spying on me the whole time. Was anything you told me true? Did you write down all of our conversations in a report and ship them off to Langley?"

Chase nods with understanding. "Isaac, every conversation was real. As I told you on the plane, I never lied to you about anything. My job was to keep an eye on the location while you were on assignment–"

Jones cuts in, "And spy on me!"

"No, that's not accurate. I was to watch for any signs of instability, and if I saw any, to report it. I never did, and can honestly tell you I have never submitted any reports about you to Langley," Chase informs him.

"What about all of your stories about your faith? Was that all just crap, were you just playing me?" Jones asks, with his voice noticeably rising.

Chase looks-up from his fruit plate, locking eyes with Jones. "My faith is the most important part of my life. It's the only thing that has kept me sane after all the years working for the Agency and then losing my wife. My hope has been that you might find your way to the Truth before you go too far down the rabbit hole, because you're going to need it to get back out when you're done."

Jones breaks from Chase's serious, almost hypnotic stare, and looks down at the table in front of him. "I understand. It's alright, Eldon. But now I know who you really are, so I know what you're up to," Jones says, this time with a small smile.

"Well, I don't think we'll be going back to Idaho."

"Yeah," Jones agrees, looking at Chase, as if in thought.

"What is it?"

"I just thank God that Michael wasn't home. Can you imagine? And Yon, why did they have to kill Yon? Why would the Lord take her that way? I just don't understand. He could have taken me. THAT I could understood, but not her," Jones says.

"Isaac, we cannot always understand why things happen in life. We have to believe things happen for a reason and still love God for what He has given us in our life. You knowing Yon was a blessing. Why she returned to heaven before you were ready to let her go will be revealed when you join her. Never forget the blessing you received by knowing her, and loving her."

"Perhaps, but will the Lord forgive me for what I'm about to do?" Jones solicits.

"What are you about to do?"

"Hunt down every last one of the people responsible for her death," Jones says without emotion, as he stands up from his seat to leave.

He hears Chase speaking softly as he walks away. Jones doesn't know if his words are directed to him, or if Chase is speaking to himself:

"We are hard-pressed on every side, yet not crushed;
we are perplexed, but not in despair,
persecuted, but not forsaken;
struck down, but not destroyed."

THE WHITE HOUSE

Chief of Staff Harrison is in his office finishing up his briefing file on Isaac Jones to give to the President before his meeting at one o'clock. His desk sits in front of the two large windows overlooking the front lawn of the White House, and he faces a wall of four TV monitors, similar to what's in the Oval Office, one for each major news channel: Fox, CNN, C-SPAN, and CNBC. He glances up every few minutes to see if there are any new reports on the Idaho incident, but thankfully, the news of the day is instead about a Senator who got himself indicted in Federal court on corruption charges. *They've moved on*, he hopes, then his phone buzzes, "Yes?"

"Sir, I have FBI Director Lee on the line," his assistant announces.

Harrison has been expecting this call to come, sooner or later. *I guess sooner rather than later*, he says to himself, and answers, "Alright, I'll take it."

He picks-up the receiver. "Director Lee, what can I do for you today?"

"I'm having a problem that I am hoping you can help me with," Lee responds.

"What kind of problem?"

"What do you know about this CIA issue in Idaho?"

"I've been briefed," Harrison says straightforwardly.

"I asked one of my agents to look into it, and I'm getting resistance from Deputy Director Waxman."

"I'm not sure what you would like me to do. My understanding is none of Waxman's people are missing. How do you justify an investigation by the FBI on rumor?"

"Mr. Harrison if–"

Harrison decides to kill the conversation before it goes any further, and interrupts, "Mr. Lee, if you are asking me to have the President tell Mr. Waxman to let the FBI nose-around based on what appears to be unfounded reporting by two over-zealous news organizations, you need to have your head examined. That just will not happen."

"Sir, if you would–"

Harrison stops Lee again, "I will not. The President holds him in very high regard. My suggestion would be to forget the whole thing and concentrate your efforts on investigations that have legs."

"Are you telling me that the White House, you, and the President, are asking the FBI to not investigate this crime?"

"Crime? There is no crime, and there is no merit to the report. If the Bureau followed-up on every newspaper story that was printed without the facts we'd have to double your budget and manpower. Should the facts change and there's suddenly something that the FBI needs to be involved in, I'm sure Waxman will let you know. So for now, I'm suggesting you spend your time on cases that require your attention, rather than on wild goose chases. We both know this isn't about a possible crime, it's about the FBI being a thorn in the side of the CIA. I won't help you, and believe me when I say that the White House is watching this very carefully. Play nicely with the other kids. Waxman has this under control. Goodbye."

Harrison hangs-up with a smile. "That was fun," he quietly says out loud.

His phone buzzes again, "Sir, Congressman Lopez is on the line."

"Lopez? What does he want?" Harrison asks, a little perturbed.

"I'm sorry, he wouldn't say. He called right after you went on with Mr. Lee. I told him you were on the line, but he asked to hold."

"Alright, I'll take it."

"Hello, Raul. How may I help you today?"

"I want you to know that I am very uncomfortable making this call, but I feel you and the President need to know," Lopez quietly but firmly announces. A long pause ensues.

Harrison breaks the silence, "Alright, I'm listening."

"I know who the source is that's leaking information about Jones to the Press."

A shorter pause follows. Harrison breaks the silence, again, "Ok, who?"

"Senator Thurston."

"How do you know?" Harrison asks, slowly sitting up in his chair.

"He told me. He said he wasn't going to let the President take 'his project' from him, so he leaked the information. I wouldn't be surprised if he tries to get the FBI digging into the mess. I think he's gone off his rocker."

"Thank you. I'll talk to the President. Let me know if you hear anything else, ok?"

"I just want you to know I am glad to be out of the middle of it, and it was never my intention for Jones to go any further than the

Benghazi mission. But Thurston wouldn't listen, it was as if he felt Jones was invincible," Lopez pauses, "…or expendable."

"I understand. You're a good man, Raul. Let us deal with Thurston," Harrison calmly says while concern is quickly building inside him. He hangs-up and buzzes his assistant, "Let the President know I need a minute before he meets with Jones."

Chapter 32

Before leaving the hotel, Jones says goodbye to Elliot
Warren, who's hurrying to catch a flight back to London.
"Thanks for being there for me, Elliot." They shake hands.

"You would do the same for me, Jonesy – maybe not as
stylishly, nor nearly as classy, but you'd get the job done
nonetheless. Although, I DO seem to be a few saves up on
you, so you owe me," Warren chides, slapping Jones' arm.

"Hey, I saved *you* back in Germany after you got shot in the
ass, remember?" Jones shoots back.

"Really, you're going to play that card again? I'm never going
to live that one down, am I ole' Chap?" Warren smiles. "Well,
I'm still tougher than you."

"Normally I'd disagree and prove it by kicking your butt, but I
have a meeting with the President of the United States, so I'll
let it pass, this time." Jones smiles and turns to the sound of
his transport vehicle arriving.

"Oh, okay, big man. Don't forget us, the little people when
you're done White House-ing." Warren smiles and walks
away, turning just slightly to get a glimpse of Isaac Jones,

unable to push away the slight, uneasy feeling that Jones may not yet be out of trouble.

The Range Rover comes to a swift stop. Jones watches as a sharply dressed agent in a tailored black suit steps out of the passenger's side and puts his right hand up to his mouth, speaking into a small, sleeve cuff mic. *Secret Service,* Jones concludes, as the man opens the side passenger door. The man, using his above-average height and piercing eyes to scan the surroundings, while also looking at Jones.

"Mr. Jones," the man says. "I'm Agent Martinez. The President is expecting you. If you would please come with me, Sir."

Jones looks at the agent and nods. Martinez turns and points to the door, "After you, please."

He closes the door behind Jones, now inside, and the vehicle quickly drives off.

They travel toward DuPont Circle, which, as normal, is congested with lunchtime traffic. However, no one can see through the Range Rover's dark, tinted windows, which intentionally conceal the occupants. The President doesn't want anyone seeing Jones arrive at the White House.

Jones is dressed casually, considering who he is about to have a meeting with. All Ms. Stella sent to the hotel was a new pair of Levis and a blue, button down, collared shirt. Jones is thankful for the casual attire. He avoids putting on a suit at all costs. Stella also sent him a new Glock 9mm with a note saying, *"I knew you would want this A.S.A.P., so I took the liberty. I'm so glad you are alright."* He smiles, reading the note, and puts the pistol in the small of his back, covered by his shirt. *She thinks of everything.*

DuPont Circle has roads that tentacle-off in all directions, as if it were a cement octopus. They're traveling on Connecticut Ave. NW. Once they reach the DuPont round-about, they have the option to stay on Connecticut Ave., or turn-off onto New Hampshire Ave. NW, 19th St. NW, Massachusetts Ave. NW, or P St. NW. The driver stays on Connecticut Ave. which soon becomes 17th St. NW, paralleling Lafayette Square, the White House, and President's Park. They pass a sign that reads, "White House Historical Association, Stewart McLaurin, President." Jones absent-mindedly thinks to himself, *Not a bad gig for Mr. McLaurin.* They turn off the road, and swiftly get checked-in at the White House Main Gate, then drive toward the back entrance.

Jones takes in his surroundings. Synonyms of the word "awesome" bombard his thoughts. Jones has never been to the White House, and has never met this President, nor any other President, for that matter. He thinks back to the Historical Association sign he just saw and of the significance of the plot of land he is now traveling on.

Arriving at the White House back entrance, Martinez opens the door for Jones, who exits quickly. The car speeds away, and Jones walks toward the door, escorted by Agent Martinez. It opens somewhat unexpectedly revealing another man dressed similar to Martinez. Jones spots a slight bump in the man's suit, confirming what he already knows... all these men are armed. Before he steps inside, the man at the door motions for Jones to stop, and says in a commanding voice, "You're not armed today are you, Sir?"

"I'm always armed," Jones answers with a tone that clearly tells these men he thinks the question is absurd.

The man motions for Jones to lift his arms. Jones holds his ground by not complying. "Listen, I don't know if you're aware of my immediate past or what I've been through the last few days, but I'm not giving you my weapon."

"Sir, we don't care who you are. You're not entering the White House with a weapon, you'll have to check it," the agent firmly counters back.

"Not a chance. Call the driver back and have him take me back to my hotel," Jones says with no emotion. Jones knows this is standard protocol, but after being taken, he told himself he would never again get into a position he couldn't get out of, without a fight. This means he will always carry his gun, *always*, even at the White House. Deep down inside he wishes they *would* call the car back. He hasn't shaken the feeling that this personal meeting with the President is *not* a good idea.

The two agents stand silent, looking at each other and then back to Jones, seemingly unsure how to proceed. "Stand by," Agent Martinez says, stepping away and putting his mic up to his mouth. Jones can't hear what he is saying. He stands smiling at the other agent, who doesn't seem impressed, or pleased, at the turn of events.

Martinez returns, looking agitated. "Let him through, I will personally escort him to the Lion's Den."

"You can't be serious!" the other agent says, in disbelief.

"That's a direct order from Chief of Staff Harrison."

The agent steps aside. Jones walks into the White House with an almost imperceptible grin.

Jones and Martinez walk down the hall together, while Jones takes in the history represented by the pictures hanging on the walls. He is walking through perhaps the most famous building in the world. Portraits of past occupants line the walls, men who changed America, and the world. They pass the offices of the Vice President and the Chief of Staff, and approach the Roosevelt Room. Jones looks at Martinez and asks, "The Lion's Den?"

"That's the code name for the Oval Office. Right through here," he motions as they enter a small waiting room. There are four desks occupied by smartly dressed women. Three of the women are on the phone, and one is seated just off to the left of a large door that Jones assumes leads into the Oval Office.

The women smile warmly as the two men approach. The President's Press Secretary, Mark Ruben, is standing next to one of the desks with some paperwork. The woman hands some papers back to him as she says, "This looks fine with me. I'll confirm with Mr. Harrison and let you know." She stands up as Ruben is walking away, "Mr. Jones, I'm Jackie; the President is finishing up a meeting and asked that I make you comfortable until he is ready. May I get you anything?"

"No, thank you, Ma'am."

"That will be all Agent Martinez. I've got him from here. I'll call you when he's ready to go," she says with a much-practiced dismissive tone.

Martinez nods and leaves the reception area just behind Ruben. As they leave, Ruben looks back and asks, "Who's that?"

"Mr. Ruben, it's not my job to inform you who the President meets with."

"C'mon, I'm the President's Press Secretary."

"So, I will assume if the President wanted the Press to know who he was meeting with he would have told you," Martinez says, turning a corner, leaving Ruben looking back toward the office corridor.

He sees Jones get seated. He examines the man for clues to his identity. *Not a politician, dressed too casual*, he thinks. *I've never seen anyone about to meet with the President in the Oval Office dressed so casually. The man is rugged, no, 'rugged' is too vague a definition. Tough, he looks very tough,'* is all that comes to him. Ruben continues trying to decipher Jones. He notes that this man looks to be in his mid-30's, and is very fit, and has a face that exudes a dangerous tone. Ruben also takes note of his above-average biceps stretching the arms of his shirt to their limit.

Ruben slowly removes his iPhone from his coat pocket. He presses the camera app, lowers his arm to his side and stealthily clicks a photo. Then the man looks up toward Ruben, as if he knows he's being watched.

Ruben quickly looks away and walks the other direction. *I hope I got his face*, he thinks as he increases his pace back to his office.

THE WHITE HOUSE

Jones remains in the small waiting room, anticipating his invitation into the Oval Office. He attempts to listen to very-well-insulated and muffled conversation coming from the other side of the wall.

The President is seated behind his desk, with Chief of Staff Harrison and Deputy Director Waxman sitting in the chairs in front of him, all engaged in a conversation.

"Lopez said Senator Thurston leaked the story about Jones to the Press because I cut him out of the Animus program?" the President asks.

"That's the story Lopez gave me," Harrison answers.

"This could turn into a huge mess if he continues. He knows everything Jones has done since the program started, and he knows Jones was grabbed," Waxman adds.

"Damn the ol' coot. He's a perfect example of why I support term-limits! Steven, I want you all over this. Tap all of his phones, including his cell. I want to know everyone he's talking to and what he's saying. I want to know where he goes and who he meets with," the President commands.

Waxman looks uncomfortable. "Sir, you realize the CIA's mandate is to operate away from the Homeland. Might this be better suited for the FBI or Homeland Security? I mean–"

The President interrupts, "Steven, I'm not asking you to build a criminal case against Thurston. I simply want to know who he's talking to and what he's saying. We need to get ahead of this. Thurston plays hardball, and at light speed. If he wants to take me on, well, I'm more than happy to pick up my best bat."

"Mr. President, something like tapping into a sitting-U.S. Senator's life without a warrant could become scandalous if anyone finds out. I'm talking Nixon-type heat," Harrison cautions.

"Then you better make darn sure no one finds out."

Harrison gives Waxman a look that says "the ball's in your court." Waxman looks back at the Commander in Chief, and says, "I could have Stella set it up from her computer, but I'll need to bring in a staff techie to help her get it up-and-going."

"I would rather not bring more eyes into this than we have to," the President says.

"I have a fairly new tech, he's still in training. He works in Transports, and he's been moonlighting on his days-off, learning tech support. He knows Jones, and they are close. He can keep his mouth shut and has learned enough by now to do something as simple as what you are asking," Waxman says.

"Fine, get it done. I only care about Intel having to do with Jones. Hold only that information, and purge the rest," the President orders.

"Yes, Sir."

"Okay, we're done here. I don't want to keep Jones waiting any longer," replies the President, ending the meeting.

The men stand and follow the President to the door. As the three men leave the Oval Office, Jones looks up, surprised to see Waxman, and he, too, stands.

Waxman walks over to Jones and they shake hands, "I'm seriously glad you're alright, Isaac."

"Thank you, Sir," Jones smiles.

The men turn, looking at the President and Harrison. "Mr. President, this is Isaac Jones," Waxman introduces.

The President shakes Jones' hand firmly. "Thank you for coming, Mr. Jones. I've been looking forward to meeting you. I'm pleased you're back in one piece." Turning to Harrison, he adds, "This is my Chief of Staff, Mr. Harrison."

Jones and Harrison shake, "Mr. Jones, very nice to meet you."

"Shall we?" the President asks, extending his arm toward the door of the Oval Office.

Jones looks back at Waxman, as if to ask if he will be joining them. "I'll be waiting out back. When you're done, I'll give you a lift back to Langley. There are a few things I need to go over with you," Waxman states.

Jones, the President, and Harrison walk into the office, closing the door behind them.

Chapter 33

Mark Ruben is on the phone with Julie Moore, the CIA spokeswoman at Langley. "I just sent a photo to your cell. Do you know who this is?"

"Okay, hold on." There's a pause and Julie says, "I recognize him. He's been here at Langley a couple of times. What's his name?"

"That's what I want to know. Jackie called him 'Mr. Jones.'"

Julie sighs deeply, "He's not a regular here. He had something to do with the Reagan operation a while back I think."

"The one where terrorists tried to bomb Margaret Thatcher's residence?"

"Yes. Jones, Jones...*Isaac* Jones, that's it!"

"So, he's a CIA spook?"

"Mark, we don't say 'spook' around here," she laughs. "Where did you get this photo?"

"He's about to go into a meeting in the Oval Office."

"Why is a CIA asset meeting personally with the President?" Julie asks.

"That's what I want to know. Find out what you can about him and let me know–"

Just then, Ruben has a sense he is not alone in his office. He turns and sees Agent Martinez and Deputy Director Waxman standing in front of him, "I'll have to call you back." Ruben clicks-off the cell phone and slowly places it back into his suit coat pocket.

"Mr. Ruben, why are you asking questions about my employees?" Waxman inquires.

Ruben panics, "Sir, I was just–"

"Your phone," Martinez requests, holding out his hand.

"What?" Ruben asks, with his mind racing, trying to figure a way out of the situation.

"Give me your cell phone, Mr. Ruben," Martinez states.

Ruben extracts the phone and hands it to Martinez, who then gives it to Waxman.

Waxman finds the photo Ruben had just taken of Jones and holds it up for Ruben to see. "Why did you take this photo?"

"I was just curious who he is," Ruben replies sheepishly.

"Who he is, is none of your business. As a matter of fact, Mr. Ruben, if I were you, I would forget he was ever here. Do you understand?"

Ruben nods. Waxman walks over to the credenza where there is a pitcher of water and four clean water glasses positioned around it. He drops Ruben's phone into the pitcher of water, with Ruben watching it quickly sink to the bottom as small air bubbles float to the top.

"The President will talk with you about this later. Take my direction, Isaac Jones was never here." Waxman and Martinez walk out. Ruben sits back in his chair, wipes his brow, and looks at his ruined phone at the bottom of the pitcher. *Holy-crap*, he thinks. The phone on his desk rings, startling him. He looks at the display, it's Julie. He lets it go to voicemail.

FRENCH ALPS, FRANCE

Mr. Hill sits at his desk in the COMMON headquarters. Just beyond the glass walls of his office, across the hall, is Brycekov's office, which security is now cleaning out. Do-hoyn Park is with them, and Hill can see him giving directions to the cleanup crew.

After packing-up all the files, they place them, along with the computer, on a cart and wheel them out. Hill assumes the computer will be wiped clean and completely destroyed. He puts an elbow on his desk, lifting his hand to his chin, deep in thought…

This group is supposed to be about international progress and the pursuit of global capitalism, helping third-world countries develop into democracies, allowing them to join the world economy.

Sure, we manipulate markets and outcomes to our benefit. Yes, we topple regimes and dictators, even start small wars, and we benefit financially from them. This place doesn't operate without expenses. But the single, most important thing has always been to benefit the world first, families and ourselves second. These two goals should be simpatico. Somehow things have turned disastrously backward.

He looks-up from his thoughts to see Park shut-off the light in Brycekov's office, and leave. Park nods at him.

How am I going to fix this? Mr. Hill wonders.

THE WHITE HOUSE

Isaac Jones is seated in a chair in front of the President's desk. Harrison sits next to him, but is on the phone. "Thank you," Harrison says, hanging-up. "Jones was right. Ruben did take his picture and was in the middle of a conversation with Julie Moore, the CIA spokesperson, inquiring about him, when Waxman and Hernandez confronted him. We'll deal with him later."

"Very good. Now, Mr. Jones, how are you?" the President asks.

"I'm fine, thank you, Mr. President."

For just a moment, Jones realizes that he's never said those words before. It's a strange realization.

"I'm very sorry about your friend, the South Korean agent," the President says with perfectly believable sensitivity.

Jones diverts his eyes, looking at the floor, "Yon U," he says reverently.

"Yes, Yon U. I understand that the two of you were close."

Jones sighs, as if to say "can we get on with it?" He looks up at the President without comment.

Harrison notices the uncomfortable pause. "The main thing is you're safe and back on American soil, Mr. Jones. Mr. Waxman has told us about you and the..." he pauses, before announcing, "the Animus Project."

Jones shifts uncomfortably in his seat.

"Well, in *our* eyes, you're an American Hero. You have served our country well, and we thank you," Harrison continues.

"Okay," Jones says rather flatly. Having a political staffer, even a Chief of Staff to the President say such drivel is clearly annoying to Jones.

The President takes over, "So, what now?"

"Sir?"

Jones gets a curious look in his eye. He has good reasons not to trust politicians, and yet this politician is the most powerful man on earth. "Sir, may I speak freely?"

"I expect nothing less from you."

Jones nods, "Alright, thank you. I don't know you. I mean, you're the President, but I don't *know* you, or Mr. Harrison here. I did vote for you, though, so there's that."

The President smiles, looking pleased.

Jones continues, "If you're asking me what I would like to do next, I would like to ask you a few questions, if that's ok. May I?"

"That would be fine."

"Do you know who was responsible for giving me up to the Russians and North Koreans? It had to have come from inside, someone working for the United States Government."

The President looks from Jones to Harrison, and nods for Harrison to answer.

"Yes, I think we do," Harrison answers.

"Who?"

"Before I answer your question, may I ask you a question, Mr. Jones?" Harrison counters.

Jones laughs, thinking to himself, *It's Just like a politician to answer a question with a question.* "Okay," he chuckles.

"I am going to answer your question, but the answer is very serious, and could have serious repercussions."

"I'd say you're right there," replies Jones. "What's your question?"

"The Animus Project, how do you feel about it?"

Jones thinks for a minute, then replies, "I think we've done some good work. We killed some of the perpetrators who murdered Ambassador Stevens and the other Americans in Benghazi. We set back North Korea's missile capabilities, and although the Reagan connection mission went a little further than I had expected it would, we saved the Thatcher residence and took out the men behind it."

The President nods and responds, "We agree. This is a pretty nasty business, and is politically flammable. Every President deals with this type of black operation, covert, out-of-congressional-oversight matters, I suppose, but it is dangerous business. Dangerous physically for the men, like you, who are on the front-line. Dangerous politically for the ones who manage it, like us."

Jones nods, "I understood all of this when I agreed to get involved."

"I know, and I appreciate that. But Mr. Jones, I'm shutting down the Animus Project. It is no more. Senator Thurston and Congressman Lopez are out. And when things cool down, I would like to talk about your future in the CIA. Right now, to put a period at the end of the sentence, I'm thinking we should all be focused on our mole problem," the President says.

"You're right on that. Right now I'm only interested in who betrayed me."

The President stresses, "Who betrayed *us*."

"What will you do when you find out?" Harrison asks.

Jones looks intensely at Harrison, his eyes say it all.

The President and Harrison glance quickly at each other, knowing the answer.

Chapter 34

Deputy Director Waxman and Isaac Jones are in the Agency's standard SUV as they depart the White House, though nothing is "standard" regarding the 35 minutes they just spent with the most powerful man in the world.

Both men are in the back seat. They are accompanied by their driver, as well as a member of Waxman's security detail who is riding shotgun.

"How did you read President Mitchell?" Waxman asks.

Jones pauses slightly, and then shrugs his shoulders. "He's, mostly believable, I suppose. But, he's a politician. I normally don't trust politicians."

Waxman nods, "Neither do I...*normally*. But there's something about him. I think he may see the big picture."

"Maybe."

"So, he briefed you on where we're at?"

"Yep."

"And?"

"McBride is a traitor. He sold-out our nation and he sold *me* out. Senator Thurston is blabbing to the Press. That is what I have a hard time with. I mean, he's the one who brought me into the project in the first place," Jones replies, almost in disbelief.

"Thurston's a politician *first*. He does what he thinks he has to do to keep his power. Don't worry. We'll handle Thurston. I've got Stella and Henry working on it. When we get enough information and present it to the White House, we'll let the President take it from there, personally. But, McBride," Waxman pauses, looking out the window, "the President said he's ours." Waxman looks over at Jones.

"How does Henry work into this?" Jones asks.

"He's been moonlighting on tech support. He's doing well."

"Alright, he's a good kid, I trust him. But until we know who we can trust inside the Agency, we can't bring anyone else in."

"Agreed," replies Waxman. Changing the subject, he says, "Stella is going to be glad to see you. She's been quite concerned."

Jones looks out the window at the blue, virtually cloudless sky and nods, "I know."

THE WHITE HOUSE

Chief of Staff Harrison lets himself into Mark Ruben's office without knocking. Ruben stands immediately as Harrison enters. Harrison looks around the room. He looks over at the credenza, still holding the pitcher of water with Ruben's phone resting at the bottom. He walks over, rolls up his shirtsleeve, and retrieves it, all the while looking at Ruben. He shakes the water off the phone.

Harrison walks over and sits in the chair in front of Ruben. He sighs regretfully, "Mark, what were you thinking?"

"I just wanted to know who was meeting with the President."

Harrison looks up at the ceiling for a moment, then back down at Ruben. "You know, I've always thought it was a bad idea to hire a spokesperson from the private sector, especially reporters from the media. The problem is, the natural curiosity you developed over the years in the Press Pool puts your nose where it doesn't belong here."

Ruben nervously interrupts, "Sir, my job is to answer the media's questions. How can I do that if I'm out of the loop?"

"No, Mr. Press Secretary. Your job is to tell the media what we want them to know, nothing more!"

"The public has the right to know–"

"Mark, you're trying my patience! You better get your head around the fact that there are some things the public doesn't need to know, for a variety of reasons."

"Like what?" Ruben contests.

"Like national security and public safety, to name two."

"Oh, come on! What does national security have to do with Deputy Director McBride being snatched? And why is a CIA black operative meeting with you and the President? Wait! Is Jones going to try and rescue McBride? Do you know where he is and who has him?" Ruben now thinks he understands, as though all the pieces just fell into place.

"What in the devil are you talking about?"

"You sent me out to lie to the media. It's my reputation on the line here."

"I did no such thing!"

"You told me there were no CIA employees missing, and I know for a fact no one knows where Trent McBride is."

"Mark, I'll start with something I shouldn't have to tell you, but this information is off the record. This is not to leave this room."

Ruben nods.

"When you told the Press no CIA employees were missing, that was true. That man, Isaac Jones…" Ruben nods, "he works for the Agency. He was grabbed in Idaho by some Russian and North Koreans. We rescued him off the Alaskan coast on a cargo ship just before your press conference. So, when you said 'no CIA employees were missing,' at the time you were accurate, we already had him back. As far as

McBride, he's not missing. I told him to take a few days off. I assume that's what he's doing."

Ruben sits quietly with a curious look in his eyes, pondering what he just heard. "So…Jones was grabbed, not McBride?"

Harrison's frustration is apparent. "Yes! The reason I didn't tell you was so when you got asked, you could honestly say only what you knew. Besides, you're going to have to accept that some things must remain unknown to you."

Ruben swallows hard. "I had no idea."

"Agreed," Harrison continues firmly and professionally toned. "Do you have any idea what kind of international outrage would occur if we publicly accused the Russians and North Koreans of violating our borders and kidnapping an American citizen, a CIA asset, no less? We didn't announce it, and that's the way we wanted it. Then, you put your nose where it didn't belong," Harrison chides.

"I'm deeply sorry."

"Indeed. Do you know how difficult it was to keep Isaac Jones from coming in here and kicking your butt after he caught you taking his picture? Did you really think a guy like that wouldn't notice? Are you crazy?! He's an extremely dangerous man who works off-the-grid. He's a ghost, and very good at his job. He was never here, and has *never* been here. The President and his staff, including you and me, have never heard of Isaac Jones. Agreed?"

Ruben pensively responds, "Yes, Sir."

Just as Harrison is leaving Ruben's office, he reaches over and picks-up the water-logged iPhone, and comments,

"Steve Jobs once said that Apple 'should make the best products, not the most.' Sounds like good advice for West Wing staff, too." Then he turns and looks at Ruben. "Now, go get another phone."

Chapter 35

Ms. Stella and Henry are gathered around a computer monitor, intently absorbing Intel. The radio's humming to Train, "Hey, Soul Sister."

> *"Your lipstick stains*
> *On the front part of my*
> *Left side brain…"*

Isaac Jones leans against the door frame that leads from the hallway into the Deputy Director's office area, and says, "Hey, Soul Sister," in a low, calm voice. Waxman continues past them into his office, leaving the door open.

Stella's eyes widen, and she turns in the direction of Jones' voice, and smiles, "Isaac Jones!" She bounds from her chair, tackling him with a powerful hug and kiss on his right cheek. She moves her lips close to his right ear and whispers, "Are you alright?"

Jones hugs back, "I'm fine, thank you."

She crooks her neck looking him in the eyes, as if to say she's not so sure.

"Really, I'm alright." He takes her hands into his, "Thanks. I know you called Warren and got the ball rolling. That saved my life, so..." Jones smiles. Their faces just inches from each other, he gently kisses each of her cheeks, first the left, then the right. Her eyes begin to well-up with tears of thankfulness. Jones lifts his hand toward her face and gently brushes a tear away with one finger.

Stella releases him, looking toward the ground, and says with a slight redness now blushing her cheeks, "Well, then." She nervously uses her hands to straighten invisible wrinkles out of her clothes, "Henry and I have—"

By now, Henry has come up behind them. "Let me get in on this group hug!" he chuckles, wrapping his arms around them both.

"Alright, alright," Jones says, clearly uncomfortable by the open show of affection.

Waxman comes back out of his office with his face scrunched up, "If you three are finished, would you mind telling me where we are on Senator Thurston?"

"Yes, Sir," Henry says, as they break from the huddle and walk back to the monitor. "We have traces on Thurston's cell and the landlines at his Senate office and home. There are three calls in the queue. After my discussion with Chief of Staff Harrison, he and I decided that I would email all collected voice files to him. He can listen to them and keep what he needs, disposing of the rest."

"Very well. What's that?" Waxman says, pointing to another field on the screen.

Henry and Stella look at each other like kids proud of some scheme they cooked up. "That was my idea," replies Stella, somewhat gleefully *and* sheepishly.

"What is it?" Waxman asks.

Henry breaks in, "This is McBride's cell phone. We're using the GPS in the phone to track his location and," as he points to another stream of data, "this field is tracking any credit card purchases."

"I didn't tell you to–"

Stella interrupts Waxman, "I told him to do it, Sir. No one knew where he was. He hasn't been home all day, so I thought, well," Stella looks up at Waxman for a sign of approval. Getting just a blank stare, she continues. "Well, I simply did what I thought you would do," she pauses, looking Waxman in the eyes. "We think he left town late last night and is now traveling on I-40, just outside of Nashville. I figured Isaac would want to know where he was when he arrived."

"You figured right. Great job, you two!" Jones says, looking at Waxman. "What's he doing in Tennessee?"

"No idea," Stella says.

"We don't have authorization for that," Waxman responds in an official-sounding tone.

"The President said it was up to us to deal with McBride. I think Stella and my boy, Henry here, have the right idea."

Jones asks Henry, "Will anyone be able to tell you have him tapped?"

"Nope," Henry says, with a goofy smile.

"Good boy," Jones smiles.

Waxman signals with his head for Jones to follow him to his office, while telling the other two, "Let me know if you get anything more on McBride. I want to know where he appears to be heading. And send Thurston's files to the White House." He and Jones enter his office, and he closes the door behind them.

Stella looks at Henry, "Do you think Isaac is all right?"

Henry looks at her with a confused look on his face.

"I don't mean right now. I mean, with everything that's happened to him."

"Isaac Jones is a rock. He's more than a rock. He's a boulder. It would take so much more than a bunch of North Koreans and Russians to break him. Don't worry, he's fine."

"But," Stella pauses, looking down, "Yon was killed right in front of him. I know he cared about her. He must be deeply hurting."

Henry reaches over with his hand, and using his index finger lifts Stella's chin to face him. "All that's on his mind right now is McBride. I'm sure he'll grieve for Yon, but not right now. His focus is on cleaning this up. *Don't worry.*"

Stella struggles for a slight smile.

"You care about him, don't you?"

Stella looks away, wiping a tear from her eye. "Of course, I do. We all do. Now don't be daft, we have work to do," she says, playfully slapping his arm.

Henry smiles, "Alright, Ms. Stella, but I think you have a little crush on Mr. Jones."

"Bugger off, Henry. You're simply a beastly young man!"

OUTSIDE NASHVILLE, TENNESSEE

Trent McBride continues driving erratically down I-40, just beyond Nashville now. He recklessly lifts a paper folded into a make-shift envelope to his nose and sniffs hard. He's long-past taking the time to carefully crush the contents into powder and use a dollar bill as a straw.

His cell phone rings. Looking at the screen, he sees, "*Unknown*." He answers, "Hello?"

Do-hoyn Park says, "Where are you going, Mr. McBride?"

"Who is this?"

"Who I am is not important. What is important is that you don't expose your relationship with our former colleague."

"You mean the one who's dead now?" McBride says with mild sarcasm.

"Yes. If anyone in your government finds out you gave him the information about Jones location, it would be problematic."

"Problematic? Seriously? He's dead! What if I'm next?!" McBride almost yells, with paranoia setting in. "'*Our former colleague*' has put me in a very bad position. He assured me Jones would be taken care of. Now I'm running for my life! I've betrayed some very serious people, including Isaac Jones. He's a dangerous man. If he finds out about my involvement–"

"Relax," Park interrupts, sounding annoyed. "Pull yourself together. Does anyone know where you are?"

"No, I left D.C. right after you called."

"Yes, I know. Where are you going?" Park asks.

"How did you know I was traveling?"

"You're being tracked."

"What?! By whom? How?" Again, panic sweeps over him.

"By those inside of your government."

"Son-of-a–"

"I asked where you are going."

"I'm getting out of the country! I'm going to Mexico, for probably the rest of my life, thanks to our 'former friend'!"

"How do you plan to get past Customs and Border Patrol?"

"Customs and Border Patrol? C'mon, they are the least of my problems. Besides, I know of a special spot that's easy to cross into Mexico just outside of Waterloo, Texas. It's an illegal crossing, but not patrolled."

Park smiles, "Good luck," and disconnects.

LANGLEY, VIRGINIA

As Waxman closes the door to his office, Jones takes-in the plush setting, and comments, "Just as I imagined it. I'm out doing the country's dirty work while desk jockeys sit in their cozy offices arm-chairing my every move."

"Isaac, I've never arm-chaired your work. You know I have always supported you and what you have done for America."

Jones pauses and nods slightly, "You're right. I'm sorry. I'm just not feeling very appreciated since finding out your boss set me up."

"That's what we need to talk about. What's your plan?"

Before Jones could answer, Ms. Stella blows through the door, "You better hear this, at my desk."

The three of them rush over to the monitor on Stella's desk. Henry looks up and announces, "McBride just took a call, listen."

Henry plays back for them the call between McBride and Park.

"I'm getting out of the country! I'm going to Mexico, for probably the rest of my life, thanks to our 'former friend'!"

"How do you plan to get past Customs and Border Patrol?"

"Customs and Border Patrol? C'mon, they are the least of my problems. Besides, I know of a special spot that's easy to cross into Mexico just outside of Waterloo, Texas. It's an illegal crossing, but not patrolled."

"Good luck."

"He's trying to skip the country." Henry announces.

"Yeah, and it sounds like he's going to try and use that location near Waterloo where we helped with that mission awhile back," Waxman says, looking at Jones.

On the U.S.-Mexico border near Waterloo there was a conflict between a Mexican cartel and fanatical Islamic terrorists. A local cop got caught in the crossfire, and Jones, along with two FBI agents, helped "cleanup" the mess. McBride knew of the mission and learned about the crossing location that to this day remains unmonitored by the United States Government.

"He must have figured that he could cross undetected, and after a few days, he could disappear," Jones says. "Who's the guy with the accent? He sounds Korean."

"No idea," Henry answers.

"It sounds like he was involved in my abduction, too." Jones adds.

"All I could get is that the call was initiated from overseas," Henry says.

"I need a plane," Jones says, looking at Waxman.

"Do I need to remind you how important it is that this entire thing be done in the dark?" Waxman states.

"No, you don't. I need a plane."

"Alright. Stella will set it up. Where are you going?"

"Gonna help another Napoleon find a new Waterloo. What's the name of that detective we helped?" Jones asks.

Waxman looks at Stella. After punching some keys on her computer, she says "Alexander Stone."

"Get me his number. Let's go, Henry," Jones says, slapping Henry on the back.

Henry grabs his jacket and laptop case rushing to keep up with Jones who is now already in the hall. "I'll link-in once we're airborne," he shouts over his shoulder toward Stella, rushing to keep-up with Jones.

Stella looks up at Waxman, "I'm worried about him."

"Don't be," Waxman replies. "It's McBride who should be worried. All hell is about to come crashing in around him."

Chapter 36

Senator Thurston rounds the corner of the foyer leading to his Senate office. He isn't surprised to see his secretary's desk empty, it was near 5:00p.m., and she has a habit of skipping-out early when he's out. After more than ten years as his secretary, he has experienced her to be a loyal aide, so he's tolerated her behavior. He enters his office, closes the door behind him, and heads directly to the credenza against the far wall. After filling a glass tumbler with ice, he fills it with a seemingly luscious brown liquid from a crystal decanter, and then swallows the entire amount in one gulp. He takes in a deep breath and exhales with a slight cough. He fills the tumbler again and walks to his desk, collapsing in the chair, as if he had just run a marathon.

"Stress getting to you, James?" says a male voice.

Thurston quickly gives a startled look toward the direction of the voice. He can barely make-out a shadowy figure seated in a chair against the opposite wall, but can't quite see the face. He doesn't need to though, he knows the voice well, Chief of Staff, Giovanni Harrison.

"Giovanni," Thurston says, as he slightly stumbles when rising. "I didn't—"

"Sit down," Harrison states emphatically, walking over to the desk.

"Don't you come in here and bark at me! I've been a member of the United States Senate since before you could walk. How dare you–"

"If you don't sit down and shut-up, you'll be completing your term in prison," states Harrison with force, as he takes a seat in front of Thurston's desk.

Caught in mid-thought, Thurston stands in disbelief and shock at Harrison's lack of respect. He starts to lift the tumbler to his mouth, contemplating his next move, wondering what Harrison knows. "Listen, Gio–"

"No, you listen. The President knows what you've been doing, you smug, power-hungry, perfect-excuse-for-term-limits, egomaniac. Just what did you hope to accomplish?"

"I'm not sure I know what you're talking about."

"You know exactly what I'm talking about, leaking the Jones story to the Press."

Thurston's face relaxes. "That's not against the law, Gio. I didn't provide any top-secret information. I didn't even give them Jones' name."

"But you put the White House in a defensive position on a story that didn't need to be reported. Why?"

"You know damn well why. If your boss thinks he can take the Animus project away from me without a fight, he's profoundly mistaken. He wouldn't be the first Commander in Chief I had to school regarding how things work in this town."

Thurston confidently lifts his glass and finishes his second drink. "Now, get out of my office before I have security remove you, you pompous twit."

Harrison remains seated, unfazed.

"This morning the President signed an Executive Order making any and all information regarding CIA asset Isaac Jones 'Top Secret Classified.' The mere mention of his name to the Press is a federal offense. You talked to three reporters this afternoon. Although it's true, you didn't mention his name, we could easily prove that it was indeed Jones you were talking about. But, hey, no need to sweat. I figure a man of your stature and age would probably only get five to ten years in the Pen. You might even live long enough to enjoy a few years of retirement, and we haven't even gotten to the illegal Animus Project, now THAT's a real story, and your fingerprints are all over it."

Thurston's eyes clinched tightly, "Is that a threat?"

"The President of the United States doesn't make threats, just policy – and he has absolutely no problem *enforcing* it. Believe me, Senator, when I tell you that he is deadly serious. Cease talking to the Press about Jones, or you will you be brought-up on charges, and he'll expose you as the mastermind behind the Animus Project. You'll be done in this town…" Harrison pauses, "…although, your future in prison will be bright."

"Using the NSA to tap my phone calls without a warrant is also a federal offense, Gio."

"Really? Can you name a phone in the United States that the NSA isn't tapped into?" Harrison smiles.

"I'm a sitting Senator of the United States."

"That's all the more reason to tap your phone, as far as we're concerned." Harrison takes a long, purposeful pause. Then adds, "But relax, we didn't get the information from the NSA."

Harrison rises and walks toward the door. Just before grabbing the door handle, he turns and says, "The way I see it, there *is* one thing you can do to get back in good standing with the President, though."

"And that would be?"

"Next week the President is going to announce his nomination for a new Director of the CIA. He would appreciate you supporting his nominee." Harrison opens the door.

"And who would that be?"

"It doesn't matter. We expect your full support, and the President *will* have it."

Harrison closes the door, leaving Thurston alone in a dark office.

FRENCH ALPS, FRANCE

Mr. Hill is in his office at COMMON's mountaintop retreat, contemplating his next move. He looks up as Do-hoyn Park enters his office with his perpetually sinister smile on his face.

"Trent McBride won't be a problem much longer," Park informs him.

"Really now? Why's that?"

"The Americans are tracking his cell phone, so I called him and got him to tell me where he was going. Now Isaac Jones knows. I expect him to be out of the picture before too much longer."

"What makes you think he'll be out of the picture and not talk?"

Park snorts, as if the question is absurd, "Isaac Jones, you don't cross a man like that and expect to just walk away."

"He works for the U.S. Government. They're not in the business of assassinating their own."

"The American Government is not as squeaky-clean as you may think. They have been assassinating their own citizens since their founding. Sometimes on their own, and on a few occasions, we have assisted, when it was mutually beneficial."

"What are you talking about? I know the Americans and much of their dirty laundry, but you say we've assisted?"

"Don't be so naive. You know our history. Long before our fathers were born, COMMON was keeping the world in order. Believe me when I tell you they do eliminate problems, just like every country does when the need arises. Do you really think JFK was killed by a lone gunman? Do you think General Patton died of heart complications after a vehicle accident?" Park can see Mr. Hill's mind churning, so he continues. "I could give you many other examples of more recent, lesser known figures, but let's just say the Clintons have had a lot of enemies mysteriously end up dead. We were even looking to help the Americans with that Snowden incident until Putin allowed him asylum. But that's only temporary; he won't be able to hide forever." Park speaks of the matters with indifference, as if the murders and implications are minor.

Hill chuckles, "How does the death of any of those people advance our cause?" Hill asks.

"You know how, financially, for political capital. The world is a game of chess, and we simply move the pieces around the board. *You know this.*"

Not enjoying this line of conversational information, Hill returns to the matter-at-hand. "So, if you knew the Americans were tapping McBride's phone, why did you call him and expose yourself?"

"Oh, I didn't expose myself. My side of the call was untraceable, but McBride told me where he was going, so now Jones also knows where he is going. It's just a matter of time, I'm sure."

Hill looks at Park with disbelief, but he knows Park is telling the uncomfortable truth.

"Cheer up, we've always been on the 'right' side of history, and we will be again when this McBride mess is cleaned up." Park turns and leaves Hill alone to his thoughts.

"You better be sure about that," Mr. Hill says out loud. He presses the speaker button on his phone and hits a speed dial button. A male voice answers.

"Yes, Sir?"

"How's our guest?"

"She's a bit bruised up, but she'll be fine. She's sleeping now."

"Good. Keep it quiet, I don't want anyone knowing she's here."

"Copy that."

Chapter 37

Isaac Jones and Henry are streaking across the nation's sky, well-above 30,000 feet, in a brand new, $60 million CIA Executive Jet Gulfstream G500. It's the jet's maiden voyage. Jones smiles as he looks out of his window, his stream of consciousness travelling almost as fast as the plane. *I grew up in that country below, was accepted to West Point, flourished there in Companies E2 and F4, got my Air Assault and Airborne wings, my Ranger tab, and have served in the US Army for all these years. I've worked under amazing commanders, and some not-so-amazing.* His smile widens. *I've worked in covert actions and commanded soldiers in war zones, and yet I never would have expected to step inside the White House and chat with the President of the United States.* Again, he pauses, looks down at his delicious dinner, scans the Gulfstream interior, and then simply laughs.

Henry stops what he's doing and quizzically looks at Jones, as if to say, *did I miss something?*

Jones smiles even wider, and just looks out the window.

Earlier in the day, when Jones and Henry arrived at the CIA hanger to board the jet, they were informed that Deputy Director Waxman had ordered the ground crew to prep this new jet for their use. The crew had just finished equipping it with all the latest communication technology. It was originally purchased for the use of the new Director of the CIA. The President suggested to Waxman that Jones break it in. Both men felt he deserved to do so.

The commanding officer for the ground crew was giving resistance to Waxman about using the jet, but Waxman simply told him, "Listen, Colonel, this is a direct order from the White House. If you have a problem, call the President and log a complaint. Otherwise, get that jet ready to fly and don't waste my time. Your passenger will be there shortly and he's bringing his own flight crew, so all we need is the pilot!" When Jones and Henry arrived, the jet was ready to go.

Jones seated himself toward the front, in a plush and very comfortable seat. A part of the seat is a tabletop that rotates forward and backward, morphing into a computer workstation with a special monitor built-in at just the right angle to avoid glare. The screen is such that what it displays is only visible to whoever is directly in front of it. The online connection is encrypted for secure activity.

Henry walks over to Jones with a hop in his step, and sets a cup of coffee down on the table in front of Jones. "Thanks, Henry," Jones responds.

"This is some plane! It makes our old bird look like something out of the 70's. The kitchen's stocked with enough food to feed a dozen people for a week! There's coffee, tea, soda, water...pretty much anything you could want. And watch this," Henry pulls a remote control out of his pocket. At the press of a button, the Bose sound system begins to play Elvis Presley's, "*A Big Hunk O' Love.*"

"Hey baby, I ain't askin' much of you
No no no no no no no no Baby
I ain't askin' much of you
Just a big-a big-a hunk o' love will do."

Henry has a huge grin on his face, and looks at Jones, who doesn't seem as impressed, "Aw, come on, this is cool, right?"

"Yeah, it's pretty cool, Henry," Jones says, smiling. "Did you find the number for that cop in Waterloo yet?"

"I couldn't find a direct line for him but I got one for his commanding officer, Captain Parker," Henry replies.

"Ok, get him on the line."

And America speeds on beneath them.

ARKANSAS, JUST OUTSIDE OF TEXAS

Trent McBride is traveling west on I-30, toward Texas, lost in thought. He wipes his bruised and red nose across his sleeve. Just a few days ago, he was on the fast track to becoming next CIA Director. Now, his career is most likely dead in the water, and he's running for his life toward Mexico. *What should I do?* he asks himself. *Is there still a way to fix this? I'll find a place to lay low in Mexico where no one can find me, and I'll contact Senator Heart, she'll know what to do.*

Suddenly, "BANG!" McBride's heart races, his eyes widen, and paranoia heightens as he ducks his head, still driving at 70 miles per hour. The car swerves off the pavement, throwing dust in its wake. Not sure if there might be another shot at him, he reluctantly moves back up in his seat, just enough to see over the dashboard, and then presses the brake. The vehicle struggles to maneuver back onto the pavement, and awkwardly comes to a rest on the side of the road.

McBride puts the gear in "park," and ducks back down quickly, grabbing his handgun from the holster on his side. He waits and listens. Hearing nothing, he peeks over the seat to look out the back window. Nothing. *How could Jones have found me so quickly?* He inspects the vehicle, looking for the bullet hole, but sees nothing.

With a curious look on his face, he puts the car back into drive and slowly presses the gas. The car feels like it is limping forward. He presses the brake and puts back into park. Opening the door, he scans the area. Finding no threats, not even another car in sight, he gets out, still holding the weapon in his hand. He slowly walks over to the passenger side and sees a flat tire. He slumps against the front fender. "Damn!" he says. "What else can go wrong?"

THE WHITE HOUSE

Senator Heart sits in the reception area outside the Oval Office, waiting for the President. Chief of Staff Harrison called her a few hours ago informing her that President Mitchell needed to see her as soon as possible. When she asked what about, Harrison said he wasn't at liberty to say, but that it would be appreciated if she would accept. Now she sits and waits. The President's executive secretary, Jackie, politely asks her if she would like a beverage, but she declines.

The door to the Oval Office opens, and Harrison bolts out as if time is getting away from him. "Senator Heart, thanks for coming," he says, approaching her with an outreached hand.

Heart stands and shakes it back. "What's going on, Gio? I've never been invited to the White House for a one-on-one with the President."

"The President would rather discuss it with you in private," Harrison says, extending his hand forward, inviting her into the Oval Office.

Heart stands for a moment, curiously considering this unique meeting, and then walks in with Harrison closing the door behind them.

The President stands up from his desk, and greets her, "Theresa! Thanks for coming on such short notice. Please, sit," he says, motioning toward the couch. They shake hands and all take seats, Senator Heart on one sofa, the President across from her, and Harrison in the leather chair next to the President.

"So, Mr. President, to what do I owe this pleasure?" she asks.

The President smiles, as if collecting his thoughts. "I've made my decision as to whom I'll nominate for CIA Director."

The Senator's eyebrows raise, she looks at Harrison, then back to the President. "I assume you're not informing all the members of Congress personally."

"No, but I wanted to tell you, personally, and ask you to support my nominee. And, actually, it's a little more complicated than that. I would like you to lead the charge in getting him confirmed. Theresa, you are a very influential person in the Senate. Having you on my side would almost ensure I get my choice through. I would consider it a huge favor."

Theresa Heart grins and studies the President before answering, wondering if he's talking to her because he is going to nominate her recommendation of McBride, or if he is going to try and convince her to throw her support in another direction. She fears the latter. Either way, she didn't plan on making it easy for him. Although she is on the President's turf, she feels as though she is in the position of power on this matter. "Well, Mr. President, if you're going to tell me Trent McBride is your nominee, you will have my full support and I will cheerlead loudly for him. I'm pretty confident we can make it happen. He's—"

The President jumps in, "It's *not* McBride."

The Senators mouth slowly closes in mid-sentence. She pauses in thought, then says, "I see what this is. You called me here personally to try to change my mind." Standing-up, she says, "Mr. President, thank you for the invite, but

McBride is my nominee, and I will not support anyone else. As a matter of fact, I will oppose whoever else you nominate, very loudly."

She starts to walk out of the room when the President stands, and says "Sit back down, Theresa. We're not done here."

"I will not. You're the President and I respect that. But you're not a dictator. You cannot tell me who I will, or will not, support." She walks to the door and turns, "Just out of curiosity, who are you going to nominate?"

"Steven Waxman will be the next Director of the CIA," the President states.

"Steven Waxman?! Absolutely not! Waxman encompasses all that's wrong with the CIA! Good Lord, Nathan, you couldn't have picked a worse person!" She opens the door.

President Mitchell cups his hands together and leans forward, "Of course, I disagree. But he's better than the traitor you're supporting," the President says softly, loud enough for her to hear, but not for the office staff outside to hear.

Heart freezes in mid-stride and turns around. Her eyes, now squeezing almost shut, and her chin tight, she slowly says through clenched teeth, "What are you talking about?"

"Close the door and come sit down. I think after I tell you what McBride has been up to, you will change your mind about him. Unless, of course, you're in on it," the President says.

Heart swallows hard, gently closing the door, and slowly walking back to sit on the couch. She realizes she just lost her position of power. "This better be good, or I will walk out that door and call a press conference telling everyone how you tried to bully me into supporting your nominee."

"Theresa, I think when I'm done you will not only withdraw your recommendation of McBride, but you will willingly support my nominee. I think you'll even agree to champion his successful confirmation."

"That's highly unlikely," she retorts, preparing herself for her own private, presidential debriefing.

Chapter 38

Waterloo Detective Alexander Stone was recently embroiled in a feud between a Mexican cartel and Islamic extremists that bled over the Texan border. With some help from Isaac Jones and a couple of FBI agents, both the cartel leader and the terrorist threats were eliminated.

Although Stone didn't get to know Isaac Jones well, he would never forget him. Stone was surprised when he got an e-mail from his superior, Captain Parker, saying Isaac Jones needed *his* help. Parker informed Stone that he should put all his cases on-hold and assist Jones in any way possible. He expects Jones to make contact soon.

Detective Stone is a good-looking man with gentle, blue eyes contrasting with his slicked-back, dark hair. He's of average height and weight, and most of the time has a serious look rather than a welcoming smile.

Stone's cell phone rings before he finishes reading the e-mail. Waiting to finish the last sentence, he finally reaches over and picks-up, "This is Stone."

"Detective, this is Isaac Jones. I was told you would be expecting my call."

"Yes, Mr. Jones, I am indeed. Good to talk with you again."

"I need your help with a sensitive issue. It has to be on the down-low, if you follow."

"I think I understand."

"There's a man heading your direction named Trent McBride. The White House has issued an 'Apprehend and Hold' order that I will be e-mailing you shortly. I'm in route, but won't land in time to collect him before he crosses into Mexico. I need you to locate him, take him into custody, and keep him on ice until I arrive. And *no one* can know you have him. Understand?"

"That sounds easy enough. Can I get my partner to assist me? His name's Jeremy Kroger."

"Yes, if he can keep his mouth shut about it. I'll be sending you a confidentiality agreement with the info on McBride. I need you both to sign it and give it to me when I arrive. It says you won't discuss this issue you're helping me with for...well, for pretty much for the rest of your life. National security stuff, not a big deal. It's on the way. I'll call you when I land."

The line goes dead and Stone almost immediately sees an e-mail arrive in his mailbox. He clicks the attachment and reads the dossier on McBride, which explains who he is and where they think he is going to attempt to cross into Mexico. His brows raise in surprise, *they want me to detain the Assistant Director of the CIA?*' his thoughts scream.

THE WHITE HOUSE

Senator Heart is, again, seated on the couch with the President seated in front of her.

"Senator, I know how you feel about Steven Waxman," the President begins.

Senator Heart lets out a deep, but somewhat sarcastic, sigh.

"More specifically, I know you think Waxman and Isaac Jones are loose cannons."

"Mr. President, with all due respect, Waxman is one thing; Isaac Jones is quite another. He should be in federal prison."

"What have you heard?"

Heart tilts her head and says to herself, *you can't be serious.* "If you don't know what's been going on with Isaac Jones since before your Administration, you're more out of touch than I thought."

The President sits up and leans in toward Heart, with a serious look on his face, "On the contrary, I know exactly what missions Jones has carried-out on behalf of the American Government, every single one. And I can tell you beyond any shadow-of-a-doubt that Isaac Jones is a patriot. The number of lives he's saved, not just here in America, but around the world, is immeasurable. There should be a national holiday is his honor, as far as I'm concerned."

Heart's mouth falls wide open in disbelief, "You can't be serious!"

"I'm deadly serious." Adding dryly, "But, a holiday is out of the question since all of his activity is top secret and classified."

The President stares at Senator Heart. "I want you to know that if any information about the Animus Project were to go public, I would be forced to have the Department of Justice investigate and prosecute to the full extent of the law. I have stamped it 'Top Secret'."

"Are you threatening me?" Heart demands.

"You're damn right I am."

Heart looks over at Harrison, "Did you hear that? He just threatened me."

Harrison holds up his hands to indicate "*keep me out of it.*"

"Relax, Theresa. I've officially shut down the Animus Project, but not because I believe it was a flawed concept. I just think it's time to move on."

"Move on?"

"Don't worry about it, let's get back to Isaac Jones. Did you know that Trent McBride gave classified information to foreign governments regarding Isaac Jones? And that this information was used to kidnap Jones, who was taken hostage from a black location right here on American soil?" the President reveals this information, while intently holding Heart's eyes, looking for a sign of awareness or deceit.

Heart's eyes drop to her lap as she processes what the President just told her. She feels a panic attack building and looks up, slowly shaking her head. "Mr. President, I knew nothing about that. You must believe me," she pauses, knowing how serious things just became. "So, the news report about a missing CIA employee was true?"

"No, not exactly, by the time reporters were on to the story, we had already recovered him from a cargo ship in the middle of the Pacific Ocean. Russians and North Koreans were holding him. They also assassinated a South Korean asset they had grabbed. Needless to say, I find this whole mess highly concerning."

"Russians? North Koreans? My goodness," Heart says, trying to fit the pieces together.

"So, my question for you, Senator, is, were you directly or indirectly involved?"

"You can't be serious? Of course I wasn't involved."

"Did McBride tell you what he was up to?"

"No!"

"I find that hard to believe," the President says, trying to decide if he should accept Senator Heart's answer. He's struck at how her demeanor had suddenly changed from angry and hotheaded, to almost soft and vulnerable. She now has a sense of pleading in her face while she looks back at the most powerful man in the world. "Theresa, I want to believe you, but considering the seriousness of McBride's actions–"

Heart jumps in, "I'm telling you, Mr. President, I knew nothing about McBride setting Jones up. I want the CIA reigned in as much as the next level-headed member of Congress, but I'm not about to give any foreign government classified information about a U.S. citizen, let alone a CIA asset, no matter how much I wish them behind bars."

The President looks from Heart to his Chief of Staff, who nods in agreement. The President rubs the back of his neck with one hand while looking back at Heart, "Well, there is a way to make me feel better about this."

A crooked smile came as she almost snorted through her nose, "Help you confirm Waxman as CIA Director?"

The President nods, "That would go a long way toward repairing the damage you and McBride have done."

"You mean, what McBride has done."

"Yes, but I think you backing him for CIA Director helped him gain more confidence than he deserved. And that helped send him on some sort of a power-trip, thinking he was untouchable. I mean, I could ask the Justice Department to look into it, as a way to clear your name, but I think my way is much more desirable, and frankly, it's cleaner. You know how information seems to leak to the Press in this city. I would hate for your political capital on Capitol Hill to decrease over something you had nothing to do with."

Heart stands up, knowing the President trumped her. "Fine, I'll support Waxman's nomination, but have no doubt, I'll be watching him. And if he crosses the line, I'll pounce on him so fast your head will spin."

As Heart starts for the door, the President stands and says, "That's fine, Theresa, but there is more to it than that. I want you to lead the charge, rallying your peers along with Senator Thurston to ensure Waxman is confirmed. Between you and Thurston, the others will fall in-line like little kids waiting to see Santa Claus."

She stops, with her hand on the door knob, and turns to look at the President, with a look of slight surrender. "Yes, Mr. President. What's going to happen with McBride?"

"Don't let that concern you."

Heart's face tightens. She realizes she really didn't want to know. "Good day."

"Thank you, Theresa."

Heart exits the office and closes the door with a noticeable slam that catches the office reception staff off-guard, but not the men inside the office.

Jackie, the President's personal secretary, gets a big grin, not making eye contact with the Senator as she passes. *She just got slammed-dunked*, she happily realizes. *Couldn't have happened to a nicer person.*

Chapter 39

After traveling on a COMMON jet from the Alps to London, Mr. Hill made a quick stop at his flat in the posh neighborhood of Knightsbridge to pack a fresh change of clothes. He then had his driver drop him at Heathrow airport where a personally chartered jet was waiting for him. If his calculations were right, he should be in the United States right on schedule. The ten-hour flight time between the U.S. and England is manageable due to the time difference, and he would gain about five hours, but it will be close.

Now reclining back in the comfortable seat of the jet as it slices through the Atlantic air, he thinks, *Things cannot continue this way. This group needs an enema, it's overdue and I think I know where to start.* He leans over the side of his chair and picks up his encrypted phone, finds the number he's looking for, and hits the call button. He knows that what he is contemplating is very dangerous and would certainly put a target on his back, probably for the rest of his life. *I'll take the gamble*, he says to himself.

The line rings and a deep voice answers, "Ethan Christensen."

"Mr. Christensen, this is Mr. Hill."

After a noticeable pause, the reply comes back, "How may I help you, Mr. Hill?"

"How's your godson?"

"I get the feeling you already know the answer to that question, but he's fine. He's about to open up a can of whoop-ass on Trent McBride. But, I assume you already know that, too."

"Yes, I am aware. I'm sure his efforts will be successful and finish a small chapter in a very unfortunate story."

Christensen, never one for exchanging pleasantries, asks again, "What may I do for you, Mr. Hill? These calls are becoming somewhat regular, I'm not comfortable with that."

"I'm wondering if we might be able to help each other."

"I'm listening."

"Not on the phone. Can we meet?"

"In person? That's highly irregular, not to mention dangerous, for both of us." Christensen says firmly.

"Can't be helped, my friend. The times in which we live have become highly irregular and dangerous themselves. Wouldn't you agree?"

There is another noticeable pause of silence as Christensen pondered the question. "Where are you?" he asks.

"Out of the country, but I should be free in a couple of days."

"How about dinner? Marcel's, on Pennsylvania Ave., in D.C., day after tomorrow, let's say, seven-thirty?"

"Perfect. I haven't dined at Marcel's in years. I love those little salmon appetizers, simply mouthwatering. I'm looking forward to it. Reserve an out of the way table, if you don't mind."

"Mr. Hill, I was the Director of the CIA. Discretion is *always* a way of life," Christensen responds as if by rote.

"I'm counting on it." They disconnect. Hill, normally a calm and collected man, wipes his brow. "Here we go," he whispers to the future.

ARKANSAS, JUST OUTSIDE OF TEXAS

Trent McBride lost a lot of time due to the flat tire. Not having all the tools necessary to change a flat, he had to call for road assistance. It took over an hour for the help to arrive, and another half-hour for the repair.

Back on the road, it took him nine more hours to get from Arkansas to Waterloo; he had forgotten just how large the State of Texas is. And the only radio station his car could pick up, a 70's dance station, was his sole companion. He spent the hours with disco greats like, Earth Wind and Fire, Andy Gibb, Thelma Houston and KC and the Sunshine Band.

The sand of time was quickly slipping past his fingers, but he needed a rest, and a shot of courage, before crossing into

Mexico. He was soon parked across the street of O'Michael's, a bar in Waterloo.

After securing his handgun in the trunk, he enters the bar. Walking in, he senses an old fashioned atmosphere. Johnny Cash fills the air with "I Walk the Line,"

> *"I find it very, very easy to be true*
> *I find myself alone when each day is through*
> *Yes, I'll admit that I'm a fool for you*
> *Because you're mine, I walk the line."*

He looks over and sees a large black man working the bar - with a smattering of patrons seated in front of him like a card dealer in Vegas. The bar is dark, and the men seated around the bar seem dark as well. When McBride walks in, they all turned around and looked at him, and then go back to their drinks. McBride walks to an out-of-the-way table and takes a seat.

The large bartender flips a crisp white bar towel over his shoulder and walks around the end of the bar, over to McBride's table. "Evenin' mister, how are ya? My name is Brown, welcome to my establishment."

McBride looks at Brown curiously, "You own this place?"

"Yup, I know, an African American owning an Irish pub, not very common. You must be from out of town. I know most folks in the area."

McBride nods.

A smile comes across the large, inviting face, revealing a row of white teeth, "What can I say…I suppose I'm just what

305

they call, 'Black-Irish.'" The big bear of a man let's his humor hang in the air.

"What can I get for you, Mr....?" Brown holds out his hand for a greeting.

"Umm, Sayer, Leo Sayer, I'm just passing through." The men shake hands. "I'll have a double shot of your best Vodka on the rocks," McBride says through a sniff of his red, runny nose.

"You got it," Brown says and walks back to the bar. He reaches up to the top shelf of the liquor cabinet, pulls down a bottle of Belvedere, and grabs a tumbler. As he scoops ice into it, he looks up at a man seated at the bar, and quietly says, "That's your boy, Kroger. He gave me a fake name, but that's him alright."

Jeremy Kroger, Detective Alexander Stone's partner, is setup in plain clothes as he sits in the bar. He and Stone had previously considered that McBride might stop for a drink before leaving the U.S. They figured right. Kroger picks-up his cell phone while Brown delivers the drink to "Leo Sayer."

With a smile and a hushed tone of voice, Kroger says to the person on the other end of his call, "Guess who just walked into O'Michael's."

As McBride sits alone at the far table, he takes a sip of his drink. His cellphone rings. Raising it to his ear, he says, "Hello?"

"You idiot!"

McBride immediately recognized the voice of Senator Heart, "*What*?"

"Did you really think I wouldn't find out what you did?"

McBride quickly wipes his runny nose with his sleeve, and sniffs hard in an attempt to clear the rest of his sinuses. "What did I do?" he asks, wanting to probe how much she actually knows.

"You gave information on a CIA asset to foreign governments? To have him assassinated? What were you thinking?!"

"Listen, we've been trying it your way for a long time and it's not working. I decided to eliminate the problem myself," McBride says in a hushed but strong voice.

"Do you realize how many laws you've broken? Not to mention how many people at the highest levels of the American Government are now on to you? You're done in this town. Don't ever contact me again."

"Theresa–"

"It's Senator Heart. Now, some might understand, in theory, why you did it, but not me. I don't agree with your methods. You stooped to their level, you stepped way over the line. You've become everything we've been trying to change and the problem is, you're not as good at this game as they are. You better watch your back. Jones is coming after you and he has the blessing of the President of the United States on his side."

"The President?"

"When the President found out what you did, he hit the roof! And now your little mistake has pushed him to support Waxman for CIA Director."

"No!" McBride screamed, not caring who hears him. He's witnessing his own personal demise.

"I don't ever want to hear from you again." The line goes dead.

McBride throws down his drink, then tosses some cash down on the table, and hobbles out the door.

Looking at the bar door, watching the stranger leave, Kroger looks back to Brown, "Here we go."

Chapter 40

Trent McBride walks like a zombie across the street from O'Michael's toward his parked car. Still, he looks up and down the street, as if checking for oncoming traffic, but is actually watching for anyone paying attention to him. His heightened drug and alcohol-induced paranoia is spiking. Satisfied that no one was watching him, he pushes the auto-unlock button and climbs in. He just sits and stares out the windshield, mindless and numb, ignoring his rear view mirror. He doesn't notice the black Cadillac sedan parked a few cars away, nor does he notice its driver, a man wearing a Fedora hat, seated and watching him intently.

Dusk is slowly falling. As he inserts the key, the headlights automatically click on. He starts the engine and mechanically puts the car in "drive."

McBride also fails to notice that as he pulls onto the road, the Cadillac discretely begins to follow behind, as the driver discards his cigarette out the window. This is one "Isaac Jones mission" that Mr. Hill wants to observe in-person. He pulls the Fedora down further towards his eyes, and slowly follows.

McBride aimlessly drives out of Waterloo and turns south on a dirt road known by the locals as Dead Tree Lane; it's not an official county road. Over time, illegal immigrants crossing the Rio Grande into Texas, to avoid immigration control had developed it from a small path into a dirt road. The road is more worn by footsteps than vehicles, over the years as its use has increased.

McBride is so close to the Mexican border he can almost taste the salty edge of a margarita glass. His car sways left and right as he maneuvers his way down the uneven pedestrian pathway, dodging around numerous holes in the dirt road, driving much faster than he should. He hopes the smugglers are done for the day. He sees a widening in the road ahead and decides to stop and get his handgun from the trunk, just in case.

As he opens the trunk and reaches in, he feels something hard press into the small of his back, and a voice says, "Raise your hands slowly and don't do anything stupid, Mr. McBride."

McBride's eyes widen and he can feel his heart begin to pound like a hammer against the inside of his chest. He raises his hands. "Who are you? What do you want?" he says to whoever is behind him.

The man reaches up and grabs McBride's right wrist, and with a swift click snaps on a pair of hand-cuffs. Then pulls his arm down and around to the middle of McBride's back. "Slowly bring your other hand down behind your back."

Doing as instructed, McBride asks again, "Who are you?"

With a click, both hands are now cuffed behind McBride's back. He hears the sound of a vehicle speed up behind them. Another man gets out and says, "That went well, let's get the package out of here before someone comes along."

As if to alert the world, McBride yells, "Do you know who I am? I'm the Assistant Director of the CIA!"

"My name is Detective Alexander Stone. This is my partner, Jeremy Kroger. There are a lot of people looking for you, Mr. McBride."

"You're local cops?"

"Not today. Today we're 'Feds', like you, working for the CIA," Kroger says, smiling as Stone leads McBride to a blacked-out Chevy Tahoe. Kroger opens the back passenger door.

"I AM THE CIA, you idiots!" McBride yells with an on-going panicked tone.

"Listen, buddy, I don't know what you've done, but this I do know: it's not the Rio Grande you're floating down anymore, its Shit Creek. I have a direct order from the President of the United States to assist in delivering you to a CIA agent who will be here soon. So until he gets here, you need to shut-up and do as you're told," Stone coldly tells him.

"What about my car?"

"You've got more to worry about than your car. It stays here."

Stone sets McBride in the back seat and buckles him in. Kroger climbs into the driver's seat while Stone sits in the back passenger seat, next to McBride. Kroger punches the gas and they quickly head back toward Waterloo.

McBride looks over at Stone, "Who's meeting us?"

"Some agent from the CIA…Isaac Jones."

The blood drained from McBride's face as he hears the answer he was expecting. *They wouldn't dare kill me, would they?* he wonders.

Kroger looks into the rearview mirror at McBride, "Man, you must be a special kind of stupid to piss-off that Jones guy. We've seen him in action. I wouldn't give two-cents to be in your seat right now."

Stone motions for Kroger to keep quiet.

As the Tahoe pulls off of Dead Tree Lane and glides back onto paved road, the black Cadillac sedan, which was parked a good distance away behind some large sagebrush, also pulls onto the road behind them, and begins to discretely follow. Mr. Hill blows cigarette smoke out the driver's side window, then flicks away the butt.

After driving back through town, Kroger increases their speed as they head north, and then turns onto a seldom-used, winding dirt road called Rattlesnake Path. About a quarter mile ahead, they arrive at a small, secluded shack that looks like it hasn't been occupied in years.

McBride looks out the window and sees the town water tower partially covering the moon. McBride sighs deeply, knowing he's in a serious situation, one he might not exit alive. Now, away from his plush life in Washington, D.C., away from the security of his office in Langley, he feels vulnerable and terrified of the man he has been trying to take down for years, Isaac Jones.

As the Tahoe pulls up to the front of the shack, McBride's eyes widen, the headlights shine on a silver Chevy Suburban parked on the side. *Company car, Jones is here.*

Kroger kills the engine and gets out. Stone pulls McBride out from his side of the vehicle.

"You realize you two will have a lot to answer for when this is all over," McBride says, losing what's left of his composure.

"Just shut-up and move," Stone says, pushing McBride toward the stairs of the shack. Stone briefly looks at Kroger, Kroger cracks a wide smile, enjoying every bit of this. Stone remains emotionless.

They walk up the creaky stairs of the old patio, and Kroger opens the door. The smell of mildew and decomposing animals fill their nostrils. Stone and McBride walk in first, with Kroger closing the door behind them. There is a dusty table against the wall under the window by a rock fireplace. There, seated at the table in one of the chairs, is Isaac Jones.

Even though McBride was expecting to see Jones, his eyes widen. Jones looks calm, mysterious, and dangerous – all at the same time. His face is half-shadowed since the only light in the room is emanating from a lantern on the table, off to the side.

"Well, Mr. McBride, fancy meeting you here," Jones says with a serious tone.

McBride looks around the room. It was just him, Jones, and the two detectives.

"Listen Jones–"

Jones interrupts McBride by immediately standing up, pushing away the chair with his right foot toward the traitor, but looking at the detectives. "Thank you, gentlemen. He can sit there," Jones motions toward the chair. Stone sets McBride down while Jones pulls out a pair of plastic flex-cuffs from his pocket and tosses them to Kroger. "Change-out your cuffs with those, please."

Kroger does so.

Jones says to the two detectives, "You can leave us now, I've got this. Thanks again for your help. I'll make sure your superiors know how helpful you've been."

Kroger looks to Stone who tosses his head to the side, motioning for the door, and they leave without another word. McBride hears the engine of the Tahoe fire-up and drive away, leaving him alone with

Jones. This is the worst of all possible scenarios, he concludes, as he slumps in the chair.

Jones stares at McBride with disgust. "You are a traitor to the United States of America."

Jones lets the words sink-in. McBride stays silent looking at the floor.

"And because of your betrayal, people died," he pauses again. "And you *also* tried to have *me* killed, you piece of shit."

McBride looks up, "Jones—"

"Did you really think you could have me killed by the North Koreans or Russians and no one would trace it back to you? I knew you were dumb, but this really takes the cake."

"Jones, I–"

Jones swiftly punches McBride in the face, causing him to rock-back in the chair. Jones catches him by the legs before he falls over. As the chair legs come back to the floor McBride spits blood on the floor. His bottom lip is cut open, and his nose, already tender and sore, is now bleeding.

Through bloody lips McBride says, "It wasn't personal."

"It wasn't personal?" Jones shakes his head. "What do you think this is, a Godfather movie? I take trying to be assassinated *very* personal! Did you know they were going to kill Yon, too?" Jones asks.

"Yon?"

"The South Korean agent who I worked with in North Korea."

McBride takes a deep breath and nods. He spits blood and a piece of a broken tooth to the floor.

Jones pulled the pistol out from the small of his back and pressed it against McBride's forehead.

"Jones! Don't! Please! I'll give you anything you want."

"You don't have the ability or power to give me anything I need, Trent. You're about to disappear off the face of the earth, and no one is going to give it a second thought."

"I'm sorry! Please!" McBride cries, tears running down his cheeks. Not because he's sorry for what he has done, but because his mind is now screaming with pain, believing what Jones just said.

Jones tightens his finger on the trigger; his hand begins to shake slightly. Images bombard his mind. He sees Yon being dragged out of the room, away from him, on the boat and he gets angrier.

Then he sees Ethan Christensen in his mind, speaking to him at Army Ranger School graduation: *"You have chosen a selfless job. Show restraint when it's needed, but don't ever hesitate when it's not. You'll do fine. I'm proud of you son."*

His eyes well-up and his face cringes, he lifts his Glock toward the ceiling and fires two rounds into the roof. *"Damn it!"*

McBride flinches, and then begins to sob.

Jones sits down in one of the chairs. Minutes pass by…

McBride gathers himself and looks up, breathing hard. "So, what now?"

Both Jones and McBride are startled when Jones' cell phone rings. He lifts it to his ear, "Jones here."

"How are you boy?"

"Uncle Ethan?"

"I heard you might need some help."

"What?"

"What are you going to do with McBride?"

Jones shakes his head, confused at the seeming coincidence, "I don't know. I–"

"I think I can help. In a minute you will have a visitor. He will be wearing a dark Fedora hat and overcoat. Hand McBride off to him and come home. He will take care of this problem for us."

"What?"

"Don't worry about Trent. Trust me, hand him off and move on, you'll be better off. Call me when you get back. Let's have dinner." The line goes dead.

Jones puts the phone back in his pocket and just as suddenly and simultaneously, there's a knock as the front door swings open. Jones sights his gun toward the door, then stops and lowers his weapon. A man wearing a Fedora hat enters, just as Christensen described.

The man smiles, "Well, well. What have we here?"

McBride fearfully looks to Jones, "Who's he? Jones? Who is this man?"

Jones gives Mr. Hill a slight nod, but doesn't smile.

"This place is absolutely horrible." Hill grabs a hanky from his pocket to cover his nose. "My goodness, I've been in some real crap-holes in my life, but this one…this is down there with the worst. Is that animal urine, or did he piss himself already?"

Jones doesn't answer.

"Who are you?" McBride asks trembling.

"Don't you know who I am?"

"No," McBride answers, his voice trembling even more. "Jones, don't leave me with this guy!"

Jones gets up. He puts his hand on McBride's shoulder, "I have a feeling when he's done with you, you're gonna wish I *had* shot you."

"Jones!"

"He's all yours," Jones says, walking past Mr. Hill without making eye contact. He starts to walk out the door and overhears Hill ask McBride, "You don't mind if I play a song by Ted Nugent, while I do this, do you?"

Jones keeps walking, and doesn't look back.

Chapter 41

Aside from the pilot, Mr. Hill and a still-trembling Trent McBride are alone on a helicopter flying low over the Gulf of Mexico, just off the Texan coast, but far enough out to sea that there is no land in sight. Hill and McBride have on headphones with a small mic allowing their voices to communicate above the loud noise of the aircraft.

McBride is strapped in, and his bloody hands are in his lap, still bound. "So, what now?" he gasps.

"This is where we part ways, Mr. McBride," Hill unbuckles his straps, removed his headphones and stands-up.

"What?" McBride pleads.

Hill opens the cargo door, and the warm, humid air floods the cabin with the scent of the salty ocean below. Hill removes McBride's headphones.

"You're going to throw me in the ocean?" McBride yells over the noise.

Hill chuckles, "Oh dear, Mr. McBride, of course not. I'm much too civilized for that. I'm going to kill you and *then* throw you in the ocean."

Hill swiftly pulls out his handgun and fires a shot into McBride's left shoulder. McBride's body rebounds back against the seat. His eyes widen as he looks at his shirtsleeve, now filling with blood.

Hill grabs McBride by both arms and stands him up. McBride looks toward the pilot, who seems oblivious to what is happening, or simply doesn't care.

Hill takes out a large knife and with a quick slash, cuts the bindings off of McBride's hands, which fall to the floor. A wind gust whisks them out the open door, wafting to the ocean below.

McBride's face is full of terror.

Hill leans in close and yells in McBride's ear, "I lied; I'm not going to kill you first." Quickly and forcefully, Hill pushes McBride out the door.

McBride's body slams into the water, and he slowly bobs back to the surface, unable to move his left arm because of searing pain from the gunshot wound. The ocean is fairly calm, but the rotor wash from the helicopter now hovering above him is creating wind and waves, disorienting him. He struggles to tread water with one arm, as blood begins to turn the water around him red. "Help!" he yells.

Hill yells back, "My good friends, the Italians, have a saying I simply love, *Arrivederci*." Hill waves an affectionate goodbye as the chopper ascends into the sky.

"Help!" McBride yells through gulp after gulp of salt water.

He looks around in all directions. All he can see is water, endless water. He's floating on his back struggling to tread water with his one good arm, looking at the clear blue sky above.

Time passes. He closes his eyes, and the world goes black, as he feels his own heart stop beating.

WASHINGTON, D.C.

Marcel's on Pennsylvania Ave. is the definition of posh. It is elegant and luxurious in an upper-class kind of way. Most of the D.C. movers-and-shakers dine here on a regular basis. When Christensen had suggested it, Hill had no complaints. He hadn't dined there in years. However, he is slightly nervous about them being seen together.

Jean-Pierre, the night manager, escorts the men to an out-of-the-way booth near the back. It is an easy seating decision, since most who dine here prefer to be noticed by fellow 5-star diners as a sign of success in this power-hungry vortex of American politics.

As Jean-Pierre leads the men to their table, he snaps his fingers at a server. She quickly arrives, already recognizing the former CIA Director, and says, "Your usual, Mr. Director?"

"Yes, please, Tina. Thank you. And the same for my guest," Christensen says, not giving Mr. Hill a chance to order, purposefully wanting to display that he is the one in control of this meeting.

"Very good," Tina says, quickly making her way back to the bar.

"So nice to have you back, Mr. Director," Jean-Pierre tells Christensen. "And Mr. Ackerley, I am delighted to see you, too. It's been some time."

"Jean-Pierre, it's simply a crime I've been away so long. The place looks magnificent, and smells delightful," Hill says in a seemingly great mood.

Leaning in close to Hill, Christensen says, "'Mr. Ackerley'?" in a hushed tone.

"One of the many hats I wear. Sometimes it's better to be known for something you're not, than something you are," Hill whispers, removing his Fedora hat and handing it to Jean-Pierre who leaves the men to themselves.

Tina returns quickly, placing large wine glasses in front of each man with what appears to be beer.

Hill laughs, "Ethan, you never cease to surprise me. What are we about to enjoy here?" Hill lifts the glass to his nose and takes in a deep whiff of the aroma.

"This is Samuel Adams' Utopias."

"Smells wonderful," Hill replies, taking a sip, smiling with approval.

Christensen tells him, "This beer is only released every two years after it's been aged for something like eighteen years in sherry, brandy, cognac, bourbon, and scotch."

"Delightful," Hill says, taking another drink.

Both men order the lamb special, and when they're finished with small talk, Hill quietly announces, "McBride has been taken care of. Thank you for your help with that. When I saw Jones through the window, struggling with his conscience, I knew I would need to intervene. Your help was vital to having it done properly."

"Do you always personally monitor operations?"

"Oh, good Lord, no. Who has that kind of time? But, I try to get out and watch the important ones when I can. It keeps me sharp. How about you? I heard that since leaving the employ of the CIA you still contract out on, shall we say, sensitive issues," Hill pries.

"Isaac struggled, did he? That's not like him."

"I think this one hit a little too bloody-close to home. I wouldn't worry."

"So, what can I do for you?" Christensen asks.

Hill lets out a dramatic and lengthy sigh. "I'm afraid my organization has gone off the rails, and is headed in the wrong direction, if you will. I want to get it back on track."

"What does that mean?"

"When I joined, it was my understanding that we would be working with democracies to make the world a better and safer place. To promote capitalism, and of course, since 9/11, to help allied nations battle the cancer of fanatical Islamic terrorism around the world. That kind of terrorism is simply bad for business."

"As is all terrorism," Christensen adds firmly.

"Oh, maybe not *all,* but that's a topic of discussion for another time."

The waiter returns with their dinner and both men stop talking while their meals are set before them.

Hill takes a bite. "Oh...my...word. To die for, Ethan. Good call, old friend."

"I didn't know we were old friends."

"Come now, I hope we will become even better friends in the future."

"I'm not in the CIA anymore. I'm not sure how I could help you, even if I wanted to. But, making the world a better place is always a goal of mine. What's in it for your organization?" Christensen asks, also taking a bite of his lamb.

Hill smiles, "Well, if we know of future events that will be taking place that we can profit on, so be it. That should not change our mandate to support and promote world democracies and stability. Unfortunately, some in my organization have become too greedy, and perhaps have forgotten that the balance between our profits and the world stability should coexist."

"Stability? I have heard *instability* is more up your group's alley."

"Ethan, sometimes a little instability creates long-term stability. A little chaos can create a yearning for order."

"And what are you yearning for?" Christensen asks.

"I'm going to create some instability inside my group…as a way of ensuring the group's future stability and order."

Christensen's eyebrow raises and he scratches his brow, "Sounds dangerous."

"Highly, but it must be done."

"And you want my help with this…what would you call it…a coup d'état?"

Hill smiles wide, "Exactly! I just love that word!"

Chapter 42

THE WHITE HOUSE

President Mitchell is seated behind his desk in the Oval Office. Chief of Staff Harrison is seated on the couch. Both men are glued to the television. The anchor announces, "Steven Waxman sailed through his confirmation as the new Director of the Central Intelligence Agency in a rare bipartisan vote."

Harrison lifts the remote control, and mutes the sound. "Congratulations, Mr. President. There's nothing quite like getting your first pick confirmed."

"Thank you, Gio. It's a happy day. Waxman will do well in his new position. What's the word on Trent McBride?"

"He's been reported as a missing person to the police. They tracked his credit cards to Texas and found his rental car just this side of the Mexican border. They don't have any leads, but think he might have run into some drug cartels or human traffickers."

"That's the official story. Unofficially?"

"Mr. President?" Harrison says, with a tilt of his head.

"You think it's better that I don't know."

"I think it's better that we never have this conversation again."

The President looks over the frames of his glasses at his old friend. "Get Waxman over here soon. I want to know his thoughts on Jones and if we should move forward with, let's see, what are you calling it now? The 'Luca Brasi File.'"

Harrison laughs out loud, "Yes, Mr. President."

FRENCH ALPS, FRANCE

Mr. Hill is seated at his desk in the COMMON compound, preparing for the all-member meeting that Do-hoyn Park had called for this afternoon.

Hill gets up from his desk and walks down the expansive hall to the cavernous conference room, which is bordered by glass walls. When Hill enters and closes the door, the walls "fog-over." All twelve seats are occupied, except his. It's rare to have everyone in attendance at the same time, considering the members come from all over the globe. Many times, members who are unable to make the trip to the Alps use video conferencing via encrypted satellite. But today, Park demanded that all be in attendance, in-person.

As Hill takes his seat, the door opens again, and two women enter, one carrying a silver tray with twelve champagne flutes, and the other carrying a matching tray with three bottles of Dom Perignon, both appear to be Asian. They are dressed identically with long, flowing, blue and black dresses, and their hair combed similarly.

"What's this?" Park asks, standing in surprise.

"I thought a celebration was in order," Hill says, motioning for the ladies to continue.

As the flutes are placed in front of each member and filled, Hill says, "The last time we were all here together was quite a while ago. I thought it would be nice to celebrate our face-to-face reunion, since it happens so *uncommonly*," purposefully emphasizing the word 'uncommonly,' looking toward Park for a reaction. Inscrutably, he got none.

Park sits back, allowing the ladies to continue serving until finished, and then they leave.

"I propose a toast. To the COMMON group," Hill says, holding up his flute. "To the future."

All the members raise their drinks to join him: "To the future!" they all say in unison, each then taking a drink.

"Now, down to business," Park says, setting his flute down on the conference room table. "Mr. Hill, it has come to our attention that you have involved yourself in a situation outside the authority of the group, sanctioning activities without the proper community authority. You know how disturbing this is to us. We strictly forbid this type of activity...and we are all shocked that you would take it upon yourself to work outside this group and put us all in danger of exposure. It's even more surprising considering the recent unsanctioned activity of another former member, who will remain nameless."

"Exactly what 'activities' are you referring to?" Hill inquires smugly.

"You rescued Isaac Jones from the North Koreans and Russians when you were instructed to keep out of it."

"That nameless former member was responsible for Jones being taken by the North Koreans and Russians. How is it in *our* best interest to do nothing?" Hill counters, remaining cool and collected.

"You were specifically instructed not to interfere. We get nothing out of it. It alienates us from the North Koreans and the Russians. The U.S. itself is capable of responding. There is no profit–"

"No profit?" Hill interrupts. "Since when is profit our primary concern?"

The other members sit quietly, sipping their remaining champagne, watching the exchange between Park and Hill.

Hill continues, "This group was formed to help keep the world secure and to support western democracies and capitalism of the oppressed. After 9/11, we voted to support the war *against* fanatical Islamic terrorists who are intent on destroying Israel, who are causing havoc in the Middle East, and who are conducting missions in western countries. Of course, my dear friends, there are opportunities to profit from our involvement, but as you rightly say, Mr. Park, this..." Hill stretches his arms out wide, "this compound, and our work here, does not come without a price tag. We have expenses that must be paid. We all understand that. Yet profit should not dictate all of our decisions. When was it decided, and by whom, that we should ignore what the 'right' thing to do is, making decisions simply based on our own profit?"

The room takes a noticeable chill.

"How dare you lecture me! How dare you lecture, us! We all know…" Park stops in mid-sentence, coughing. He clears his throat, raising his hand to his neck and looks down at his glass. His body seems to tremble in his chair and his head suddenly hits the table with a crashing thud. The other members start coughing, much the same as Park.

Panic takes-over the group, chairs getting pushed back in haste, men and women falling to the ground, grabbing their throats, choking, and gurgling in their own saliva and blood.

Then silence.

Hill picks up his champagne glass, and lifts it high. "Cheers."

The door opens and one of the Asian women who helped serve the champagne, enters, with Ethan Christensen on her heals.

Christensen says, "Interesting…it went just like you said it would."

Hill smiles, "Why wouldn't it?" He rubs his hands together.

Hill states, "Now we rebuild this group from scratch. With your contacts around the world, we should be able to fill these chairs with like-minded replacements in no time."

"What about their sponsors? Won't they expect to inherit the vacant seats?" Christensen asks.

"No."

"That means there are eleven people on the outside who pose a threat, simply by what they know."

"I've arranged small stipends for each of them to keep their mouths shut, accompanied with a threat of retaliation if they go public," Hill smiles. "Money and fear mix well, it seems. Always has, always will."

Christensen nods.

"And you, my new friend," Hill takes the Asian woman's hand, "you will be comfortable here, too," Hill politely kisses the top of her hand.

"Well, it seems our next task at-hand is letting Isaac Jones know you still grace the earth."

Yon nods, and blushes.

Christensen concurs.

"Alright then. Let's get someone in here to cleanup this mess, shall, we?" Hill says, motioning to the door. As they walk out, Hill stops, turns, and looks around the conference room. He eyes each now-deceased member. He raises his champagne glass to the dead, and says, "To new beginnings."

Epilogue

Isaac Jones is seated on the porch of his new townhouse, just outside Washington, D.C. His son, Michael, home for the weekend, was thrilled when his dad picked him up from school earlier in the afternoon, letting him know that he now lives closer, and they would be spending much more time together.

Michael is on the computer playing some kid's game, after Jones had checked to make sure it was appropriate for a young boy.

Dinner is over, and Eldon Chase is seated in the chair next to him.

"How are the new digs?" Jones asks.

"Same as yours, kind of sterile, but I'm making it a home. I'll have to plant a new garden, and the grass has been neglected. I'll also have to find a new church, but I can make it work. I have to tell you, after what happened, I was surprised they kept me on as your house guardian."

Jones lifts his can of beer and the two men bump them together. "I told them I wouldn't have it any other way."

THE WHITE HOUSE

It's now after 7:00p.m., and President Mitchell is late for dinner with his wife. But he wants to finish reviewing the report Harrison prepared for him.

He perused the single page that sits inside the black, leather folder with the Presidential Seal on the front. He studies it again, for the third time. Then he takes off his reading glasses, rubs his eyes, and sets the folder down. He sighs, and reads the title of the page again, "Code Name - *Invisible Man.*"

He closes the leather folder, and walks out of the Oval Office, glad to be done for the day, and now looks forward to dining with his bride.

~ The End ~

Also By Ryan Pacheco

Benghazi and Beyond-
(An Isaac Jones Thriller)

The Heist-
(An Alexander Stone Thriller)

Earth's Dimensions-
(The Forbidden Woods)

Earth's Dimensions-
(The Portal)